ONE WITCH TOO FEW

ONE WITCH TOO FEW

THE WITCH NEXT DOOR™ BOOK ONE

JUDITH BERENS

LMBPN Publishing
PMB 196, 2540 South Maryland Pkwy
Las Vegas, NV 89109

First US edition, August 2019
ISBN 978-1-64202-410-4 (ebook)
ISBN 978-1-64202-411-1 (paperback)

ONE WITCH TOO FEW TEAM

Thanks to our beta readers

Nicole Emens, Mary Morris , Larry Omans, John Ashmore, and Kelly O'Donnell

Thanks to the JIT Readers

Deb Mader
Dave Hicks
Peter Manis
Dorothy Lloyd
Jeff Eaton
John Ashmore
Paul Westman
Micky Cocker

If we've missed anyone, please let us know!

Editor
SkyHunter Editing Team

DEDICATIONS

From Martha

To everyone who still believes in magic
and all the possibilities that holds.
To all the readers who make this
entire ride so much fun.
And to my son, Louie and so many wonderful friends who
remind me all the time of what
really matters and how wonderful
life can be in any given moment.

From Michael

To Family, Friends and
Those Who Love
To Read.
May We All Enjoy Grace
To Live The Life We Are
Called.

ONE

The business card in Lily Antony's hand glowed with a gentle purple light. Neon-purple fireworks burst around the edges of the card and illuminated her face with the harmless sparks that escaped. Every three seconds, the gold-trimmed words *Le Chapeau Magique* scrolled across the card, replaced by a new phrase—*Goûtez à vos rêves les plus extravagants.*

"Taste your wildest dreams," she muttered. "Why don't I remember this?"

Across Meeting Street from the parking garage where Lily had lived temporarily out of her 2002 Winnebago Adventurer, a man in a gray business suit summoned a ball of green fire in his palm.

Lily waved a hand over the hunk of broken metal that had gotten into the box of her mom's things, but her spell didn't reveal anything hidden there. *It's only a piece of junk. But it can't be.*

The man entered the parking garage and moved a little closer to the RV.

"I know there's a reason, Mom." Lily stared at all she had left of the witch who'd given her life and taught her everything she could. "Nobody wants to believe me."

A loud, firm knock on the side door of the Winnebago distracted her. With a frown, she put everything in the box, slid the lid on, and shoved it under the bed in her cramped bedroom. The knock came again. "Coming," Lily called. "I know I'm almost paid up for parking here. What do they want?"

She crossed the RV and walked down the two steps to open the door. No one was there and she stuck her head out to look around. "Hello?" *Either kids are dingdong ditching RVs now, or I'm hearing things.* The second she stepped fully onto the cement floor, she saw the bright green flash on the other side of the garage. It hurtled toward her at an incredible speed.

Lily darted to the side and the fiery green missile barreled past her, through the doorway, and into the ugly floral couch inside. Her gaze locked onto the unexpected aggressor, who stalked toward her with purpose. More green fire was already building in his hand.

In broad daylight? Is he crazy? "Hey! You almost—" Another fireball streaked toward her and she ducked before it left a charred dent in the outside of the Winnebago. "You got my attention," she yelled. "What do you want?"

The man's next attack convinced her that he definitely didn't want to talk. Before he could hurl another assault,

Lily thrust a fist at him and opened it, palm upward. Her spell dumped a bucketful of water onto the man's hand and instantly snuffed out the new flames. He glanced at his dripping palm, then raised the other toward her. A red, sparking bolt of light burst from his fingertips.

She was ready for it. Her next spell deflected his attack with a bright yellow shield halfway before it reached her. The red sparks dissipated, and the man began to run toward her.

"Crap, crap, crap..." She scrambled around the Winnebago to put it between them. The RV rocked violently when another spell struck the other side. "Stop it! I live here." *That's probably what he came to change.* Lily leapt toward the driver-side door, jerked it open, and clambered up into the driver's seat. The engine started with a quick turn of the key. She yanked the door to close it but her assailant grasped the edge and held it open.

He sneered at her and cocked his head. "Nothing personal. We're merely cleaning up loose ends."

Her instinct enabled her to react much faster than he did. She released the door and delivered a shimmering blue wave of a stun spell directly at his head—close enough that she couldn't possibly miss. He looked like he was about to sneeze, but his eyes rolled back in his head and he fell like a stiff board. His head struck the concrete floor with a crack that made her wince. "That was personal. Sorry, but at least you won't remember the last twelve hours when you wake up." She pulled hard again on the door to slam it shut, put the Winnie into reverse, and tried to drive like someone who hadn't just been in a witch fight in the middle of downtown Charleston where anyone could see.

Almost being burned to a crisp didn't exempt her from having to stop at the tollbooth. She owed ten bucks for parking there overnight and half the day. Before the Winnebago rolled out of the garage onto Meeting Street, a shadow passed over the unconscious man in the gray suit. The bird pin on his jacket flashed bright silver and he disappeared.

Traffic was light on the quick drive through the heart of downtown. It gave her enough opportunity to check her rearview mirror and both side mirrors every few seconds— for witches instead of other cars. "That guy came out of nowhere. What did he mean by 'cleaning up loose ends?'"

Only when she pulled onto Ashley Avenue did she realize what she was doing. "Okay, Romeo's all I have left." Lily nodded and took a deep breath. "It's worth another shot now that someone tried to kill me."

The Winnebago pulled up in front of the house she hadn't visited for seven years, and Lily cut the engine. After she smoothed the last strands of blonde hair away from her face, she pulled her keys out of the ignition, stuck them in her purse, and stopped. *Yeah, I need shoes.* She went briefly back to her room, grabbed the first pair she saw, and shoved them on. *I'm not gonna hunt for the right pair when I know someone's after me. I only hope they didn't follow me here.*

The RV side door creaked open and she took another quick glance in either direction. Every car on the street was parked and there was no moving traffic. The few people out there walking around midday in a Charleston summer were heading away from her. *So far so good.*

"You can do this, Lily." She tried to keep it together as she stepped up onto the sidewalk, not wanting to draw more attention to herself than the Winnebago had already done. Her attempts were successful until she tripped on some scattered mulch that had escaped the garden in front of the porch. By the time she stood at the front door and her finger hovered over the doorbell she'd rung hundreds of times as a kid, Charleston's muggy summer heat had already gotten to her. Her blouse felt damp, and the hair at the base of her neck clung to her skin.

We're still friends. Lily nodded to encourage herself and rang the doorbell. *Maybe this time, he'll want to see me. I really need him to see me.*

Footsteps grew louder from inside the house, and the next second, she peered through the screen door at a man she almost didn't recognize. He opened it and stared at her. "Lily," he said, and he definitely didn't sound happy about it.

"Wow." She swallowed and studied him with a mixture of curiosity and appreciation. "Hi. You look..." *Amazing.* Dark, curly hair tumbled over Romeo's forehead and almost into his green eyes. There was a lot of muscle in his tanned arms and not much left to the imagination beneath his white t-shirt, and he was probably a foot taller than the last time she'd seen him. "It's been a while, huh?"

Romeo chewed on the inside of his cheek and glanced across the street. "What are you doing here?" he asked.

"I..." She forced a smile, then turned to double-check the street again. "Can I come in?"

He returned her scrutiny before he responded, and a small frown settled over his features. "Yeah." He held the screen door open and stepped back to let her inside. They used to barrel through that same door together when they were kids. Now, she had to turn sideways to skirt past him. He hesitated for a few seconds and peered out into the street, then turned to look at her. "Did you see anyone get out of that Winnebago?" He jerked his head toward the open door.

Lily's eyes widened, and she tilted her chin. "Uh...yes. Yes, I did." He cocked his head in confusion so she added, "It was me."

She expected him to laugh, but he merely frowned at her and licked his lips slowly. "Not really your style these days, is it?"

"Well, no. It's—"

Romeo let the screen door bang shut and closed the front door again before he stepped past her into the living room and plopped down on the couch. Lily followed and scanned the pictures of him and his family on the mantle over the fireplace where they'd always been. The brown and green dartboard still hung on the wall beside it too. "Have a seat," he told her.

When she chose the other side of the couch, he scooted away a little and draped his arm over the armrest. *Maybe I should've picked the La-Z-Boy.*

"How've you been?" she asked. He took a deep breath through his nose and simply watched her and waited, so she decided to dive in. "I wanted to call first, but I guess your parents got rid of the landline, huh?" He blinked at her. "Romeo, the last couple months—"

"Did you get my letters?"

She froze. "What?"

"I know I sent them to the right address," he said and his frown deepened. "I double-checked."

Lily sighed. "Yeah, I got your letters."

"Did you read them?"

"Romeo—"

"Did you?" He inclined his head to stare at her so intensely, she couldn't think of anything to say.

She glanced down at her lap. "Yeah, I read them."

"So you know they put me in jail for something I didn't do, right? And you know that I spent months in that jail trying to clear my name. My dad spent almost all his retirement money on a good lawyer to get me out of there, and you...what? You couldn't step out of your fancy colonial to help a friend?"

"Okay, I didn't come here to start a fight." Lily took a deep breath. "But don't pretend that what you did was my fault."

"I wrote you five letters," he added. "I remember that because they sell stamps at the commissary five at a time on a little strip. That was all I could buy if I wanted paper, too." He huffed out a breath of disbelief and ran his hand through his dark curls. "I know we haven't seen each other in a long time, but you were the only person I wanted to talk to when I thought I was gonna be locked up for five years. For something I didn't do. I needed you, and you..."

He shrugged and dropped his hands into his lap. "Did you simply not care?"

"Of course I cared," she said, her cheeks burning now. *Why is he doing this?* "I still care."

"Then where were you?"

"I was there, Romeo." This time, she shouted because he really seemed upset. *If he'd actually wanted me there, he shouldn't have turned me away.* "No, I didn't get your letters right away. My mom and I were..." She swallowed. "We were helping out some fairies at a shelter for displaced magicals up north." *And that was the last real quality time I spent with her.* "Your letters were waiting for me when we got home, and I drove right up to County to see you."

Romeo blinked. "No, you didn't."

Lily's cheeks felt even hotter than before. "Every day for two weeks. They kept telling me you hadn't put my name down on the visitor's list. I don't know why you wrote me those letters if you didn't really want me to come. No, I didn't show up when you sent the first one, but I swear I would have if I'd been home. Two weeks is kind of a long time to punish me for that, don't you think? Eventually, I stopped trying."

His jaw clenched and unclenched over and over as he stared at her. After a snort like an angry bull, he shook his head. "It takes so damn long for anything to process in that place."

"What?"

"I filled out two requests to put you on that list. Because I wanted you there."

"You did?" She uttered a breathless laugh when he pressed his lips together and nodded slowly. "I thought you changed your mind. Or that you were still... angry because I couldn't spend as much time with you as I used to."

It took him a minute, but he finally leaned toward her and didn't look so reluctant about it. "You think I grew up and suddenly became a jealous person out of nowhere?"

"I didn't know what to think. Romeo, I am so sorry that you had to go through that on your own."

He chewed the inside of his cheek again. "None of it was your fault. I can't believe you made that drive every day for two weeks."

Lily chuckled and shrugged. "I really wanted to be there—" A car door slammed outside and jolted her back into the reason she'd come here when she still thought he hated her. Her head whipped toward the front door.

"What's going on?"

"Well..." She bit her lip, turned hesitantly toward him, and tucked her hair behind her ear. "I hope you'll believe me because this time, I was actually attacked by the people whom I think are trying to keep me from the truth."

TWO

"Wait, *what?*" Romeo bolted to his feet and stormed across the living room to peek slowly through a small gap in the curtains. He turned to face her and asked, "Someone attacked you?"

"Right out in the open. For every non-magical to see."

"Are you okay? Did they hurt you?" This time, when he returned to the couch, he didn't think twice about sitting down so close beside her that their knees touched.

Lily swallowed and couldn't help the tiniest smirk. "Of course I'm okay. I can handle myself. And when he wakes up, he's not gonna remember that part, either."

He chuckled, then instantly cut it short and looked embarrassed. "That doesn't surprise me at all. What did you do to him?"

"I gave him the chance to be civilized and talk it out. That wasn't his style, I guess. He got a little too close and I hit him with a stun-memory-wipe combo." She shrugged and raised her eyebrows.

His eyes were wide as he took that part in. "Of course you did. You said they're trying to keep you from the truth."

"Yeah, okay." She shifted toward him and pulled her feet up to cross her legs on the couch. He turned, his head tilted toward her. *Like we're nine again and telling scary stories in the dark.* "I need you to try to wrap your head around this. Because no one else—and I mean no one else—believes me." She stared into his bright green eyes and exhaled a slow breath. "I think my mom's still alive."

"Lily—"

"I know, I know. Just listen. I promise this isn't denial or grief or anything like that." *Whatever he's about to call it, I've heard them all at this point.* "Her death was made public, right? College of Charleston's acclaimed professor of antiquities pronounced dead."

"Hey, I'm so sorry I never called—"

"No, no. It's not about that." Without thinking, she reached out and grasped his hands. "Let's call it even, okay? You thought I didn't want to come see you. I thought you didn't want me there. We were both wrong. I wanna throw that under the rug." She bit her lip and studied his gaze.

Romeo glanced at her hands in his and swallowed thickly. "Okay."

She removed her hands and clasped her crossed ankles instead. *That was a little too much.* "So they pronounced my mom dead and had a big old service and everything. It was awful, by the way—not in any way what she would've wanted, which was totally weird. Then, a lawyer I've never seen before showed up at our house to read me her will. I guess you don't really need a body for either of those things."

"Wasn't she a little young to write a will?"

Lily shrugged. "Well, my mom liked to prepare for everything. That part wasn't weird. But she would never write something that cut me off completely."

He frowned. "Cut you off as in no inheritance, or—"

"No, I mean everything. Right, no inheritance. But they took our house and our cars, and seized all our accounts. Then they came through and helped themselves of everything of any value." She scoffed and shook her head. "They gave me a week after that to take whatever I wanted from what was left before I was out on the streets."

"That's insane."

"I know. My mom wouldn't do that, Romeo. Everything she did, she did for me. Okay, and because she simply loved the thrill of it. But we didn't have some giant fight that would make her do this before she disappeared. Nothing any bigger than normal fights, anyway." She swallowed and hunched her shoulders before she lowered them slowly and deliberately. *Here comes the big one. Buckle up.* "So I think someone faked her will. I think she went missing on one of her adventures and someone's trying to cover it all up."

Romeo rubbed the back of his neck and scowled. "Or she was taken."

"Exactly. Oh, my God, you have no idea what a relief it is to hear you say that." Only when he scooted even closer and wrapped an arm around her did she think she might possibly cry. *But you're not done yet.* "Nobody believes me, Romeo. Not her real lawyers or her coworkers at the school. Our old neighbors pretend they don't even know me. They made everything about her death their business until I asked for help. And I would've had the money to prove it—to find something to prove it—if that wasn't all gone too."

"I believe you." He fixed his gaze firmly on hers, squeezed her shoulder, and gave her a little jostle of reassurance. "I knew your mom well enough to know none of it sounds like her."

All the tension flooded out of her. "Thank you. Really. I would've gone to her lawyers again, maybe, but the only vague proof I have is a witch in a gray suit who tried to kill me with fireballs and seriously strong attacks. None of them are witches, so that's a little impossible."

"Right." He rubbed her arm gently before he removed his from around her shoulder and scratched behind his ear. "Why do you think he tried to kill you?"

"Beyond the obvious attack?" He shrugged and Lily closed her eyes to bring up the witch fight she almost wished she could forget. "For starters, he told me he was merely cleaning up loose ends."

"You're kidding."

"Nope. Of course, he only said it 'cause he thought he had me, but I knocked him out."

He obviously tried hard not to laugh. "I would've loved to see that."

Lily smirked. "Well, thanks. I think it bought me time. A day, at most, depending on when he wakes up."

Staring at each other like this was apparently a little too intense for him. Romeo looked away and frowned. "So you got rid of the guy who tried to kill you, and you're still a little jumpy. My guess is that it's not aftershock with you."

"Nope. I think there's more than only one guy."

"That sounds about right."

"He said 'we.' It's the first time someone actually attacked me, though. And I wasn't even doing anything. I've run around for two months since the funeral and tried to convince someone to believe me. And today, I—" *Oh, my God. That's it.*

"Lily?"

I knew I'd never seen that business card before. She must've put it in the photo album.

"Earth to Lily."

I still don't know about the broken metal, but I definitely didn't put it in that box. What were you trying to tell me, Mom?

"Lily Antony, snap out of it." The harsh click of his snapped fingers right in front of her face broke her distraction.

She pulled back a little, blinked at his hand, and turned to raise her eyebrows at him. "What?"

"I think this is the part where you tell me where you just went."

"Oh. I think I found some clues my mom left me. Something she wanted me to see so I could look for her if anything...happened."

"Yeah, that sounds like your mom." Romeo squinted at her. "Are you sure they're clues, though?"

"Well, the fact that I've never seen them before in our personal stuff is a start. How 'bout the day I find them, a random witch throws spells at me in a parking garage? That's too much of a coincidence. And my mom raised me on puzzles and scavenger hunts. I know what they feel like."

"You're gonna follow the clues, aren't you?"

Lily laughed in surprise. "Was that a real question? Of course I am."

"And you're gonna take me with you."

She frowned, glanced at the front door, and directed her gaze right back to him. "No."

"Lily, you can't—"

"Let you get involved in this mess? You're right." She stood abruptly from the couch and paced toward the mantel over the fireplace. *He's always been there for you, Lily. Even when you thought he wasn't. And Romeo's literally the smartest person you know besides Mom.* Slowly, she turned to see him lounging quite comfortably, his ankles crossed on the carpet and one arm slung over the back of the couch. *Because he knew I'd reconsider.* "Okay, for starters, you know this will probably be really dangerous, right?"

"Yep."

"And we might end up in trouble. Or worse."

"Two heads are better than one." He leaned forward to rest his forearms on his thighs.

She sighed. "If you don't wanna come, you don't have to. I can totally do this on my own."

"I know."

She crossed the living room again and stopped directly in front of him so he had to crane his neck to look at her. "I need you to think really hard about this, because I don't want to see you hurt because you feel you have to protect me."

Romeo stood slowly, so close in front of her that their noses almost touched. Now, she had to look all the way up to hold his gaze. "Have I ever lied to you?" he asked.

"No."

"Do you want me to come with you?"

A laughing sigh escaped her when she realized the answer. "Yes."

"Do you trust me, Lily?"

I literally didn't know until we resolved that giant paperwork snafu. "A hundred percent."

"Then I'm coming with you."

Finally, she nodded and squared her shoulders in determination.

Romeo shrugged. "You know what? I think we might actually be the first ever witch and werewolf team."

"Have you ever fought against magic?"

He smirked at her, and the heat radiated off his chest in the surprisingly tight t-shirt. "Only yours. But trust me, I can take more than you think."

Her gaze flickered over his huge muscles as he folded his arms. "I bet you can." Lily swallowed. *Focus.* "But if you end up thinking you're in way over your head, I won't be mad at you if you back out."

His grin looked entirely feral. "Don't ever say that again."

A shiver ran down her spine, and it wasn't out of fear. *Man, he really grew up.* "Point taken."

Romeo leaned over the arm of the couch, opened the drawer of the side table, and withdrew a handful of silver rods. They clinked against the tabletop before he shut the drawer and picked one up.

"Um..." Lily spoke as he turned back toward the mantel. "I'm not sure your darts are gonna help us figure anything out."

"I'm thinking." He raised his hand, the black-and-green flights level with his cheek, and squinted as he aimed. "Tell me about the clues."

"Okay. The first one was a broken piece of metal but I still don't know what it means. The other's a business card. It...glows. And the words in French keep changing."

He sent the first dart into the center of the bullseye. After a quick glance at her, he nodded, picked up a second dart, and lifted it to throw again. "Keep going."

Lily blinked. *How can he focus at all with that thump?* "'The Magic Hat' and 'Taste your wildest dreams.' That's what it says. And there's a bird and the sigil for the Order of North, but I can't—"

Romeo released the second dart and it stuck home and quivered beside the first one. "What's the Order of North?"

"It's a society that—oh."

"Oh?"

"That actually works with the thinking part."

He chuckled and studied her face. "Yeah, I know. Wanna share the revelation?"

"You uh...keep throwing and thinking. I realized I know someone who might be able to help, so I'm gonna make a call." She tilted her head and stared at him. *Is he sure he actually wants to do this with me?*

Romeo shrugged. "Okay."

"Okay." She turned and moved toward the kitchen as she drew her phone from her purse.

"Lily?"

"Yeah?"

"I'm really glad you showed up." It was as hard for him to say as it was for her to accept.

She knew that because he didn't quite smile at her. *Thinking we turned on each other still kinda stings, huh?* "Me too," she said and left him to his darts while she made the call.

THREE

"Bentley McClure. This is Melissa. How can I help you?"

"Hi, Melissa." Lily turned away from the living room to stare at the pictures of Romeo and his dad on the fridge. "It's Lily. Is Bentley available?"

"Just one moment, Ms. Antony."

"Thanks." She traced her finger down the ceramic magnet of South Carolina's iconic symbol—a palmetto tree with a crescent moon rising on its right. *I had this on a t-shirt. What happened to it?*

"Lily?" Bentley's voice startled her from the memory, and she knocked the magnet off the fridge. It clattered to the floor and two different pictures floated down behind it.

"Hi, Bentley. How are you?"

"I'm fine. Just fine. How 'bout you?"

"I'm...well, I've been better, actually. A lot better."

"I can tell. Did something happen?"

"Kind of." She bent down to the floor, her knees

pressed tightly together within her cream skirt, to retrieve the magnet and both photos. "I think I found something of Mom's."

"That the bank didn't take?"

"Yeah...more like something I think she wanted me to find."

The soft shuffle of papers came through the other end of the line. "Lily, I know how hard this is to accept. I was as surprised as you were to see the terms of her will unfold the way they have. But there's nothing we can do about it."

"Okay, be honest with me. Do you really think she wrote that will herself? That she'd take everything away once she was gone?"

Her mom's accountant and family friend drew a sharp breath, then sighed. "Not that she'd take everything away, no. But you and I both know Greta did things in her own way for reasons that are often impossible to understand."

"That's exactly what I'm talking about." Lily tucked the phone between her ear and her shoulder and flipped the palmetto magnet absently over and over in her hands.

"That doesn't mean she's still alive."

"How about the fact that a witch I've never seen before tried to kill me less than an hour ago? Right out in the open with no illusion wards."

"What?"

"He told me, 'We're merely cleaning up loose ends.'"

Bentley whispered quickly into the phone, "Lily, I told you when I gave you the keys to the RV that you needed to get out of town. I have no idea what's going on, but it's clearly not safe for you to stay."

"I know. And I think I found some clues my mom left me that will help me to find her. I need your help to decipher what they mean."

She heard the man swallow over the phone. "What kind of clues?"

"We probably shouldn't talk about it over the phone. Can I meet you somewhere?"

"Lily, you know you're always welcome at the office—"

"No, no. Not your office, Bentley. If there are more of them after me, I don't want to get you sucked into this. Just somewhere...normal. Public."

"McGrady's Tavern at 5:30. I'd say screw the paperwork, but this client doesn't give a lot of wiggle room. Can you be there in half an hour?"

"Of course I can. And I'll bring a friend."

There was a long pause. "I hope it's a friend you can trust."

"Exactly like you, Bentley." Lily let herself smile, knowing she at least had two people who were completely on her side. "There isn't any other kind of friend."

"Okay. Stay safe. I'll see you soon."

The call ended, and she slid her cell phone into her purse and turned her attention completely to the magnet and the photos. The first photo she pressed against the fridge had to be recent—Romeo and his dad Julian on a small fishing boat down in Edisto. *Or maybe Beaufort. God, it's been so long, I can't remember.* They both held up a huge fish and grinned into the sun. She stuck the magnet over the photo and looked at the second one.

Oh, my God.

Lily was eleven years old in this picture, and Romeo was twelve. He was scrawny and pale and her belly looked a lot chubbier than she remembered it in that neon-green bikini. She hadn't been overweight as a kid, but she hadn't been as sticklike as Romeo. *That's only because we were sitting down*, she reasoned. Julian had taken this picture while both kids were eating watermelon on the dock, half turned toward the camera with juice dripping down their chins. She laughed to see the black watermelon seeds stuck to Romeo's chest. Looking for the spot on the fridge where this might've been, she remembered it had fallen with the magnet. *Did he really cover this one up?*

"Any luck?" Romeo called from the living room. Another dart thunked into the board.

"Uh, yeah." Lily stuck the corner of the ten-year-old photo beneath the magnet where it wouldn't block the fishing shot, then left the kitchen. "We're meeting him at McCrady's Tavern. Five thirty."

Romeo raised an eyebrow. "Public place. Good choice. I've never been there."

"Really? Well, we're not really going there to eat. But I promise we'll find a restaurant equally as good somewhere."

"Whatever. I merely like food." He smirked and aimed the fifth and final dart at the board, and she stepped up beside him and held her hand out.

"Do you mind if I try?"

He studied her with a small smile, then stepped back and handed the dart to her. "When was the last time you threw one of these things?"

"It's been a hot minute, actually. Thanks." Lily adjusted her position, lifted the dart, and closed one eye while she took aim.

"You're holding it wrong—"

"I am not." When she threw with her right hand, she flicked the air with her left. One of the four metal shafts stuck in the board dropped with a clink before hers took its place in the bullseye.

He snorted. "That's cheating."

"What?" She spun to face him and put a hand on her hip. "Prove it."

He leaned toward her and flicked the air between their faces. "Magic."

She laughed. "There's no way your wolf power doesn't get any credit for those bullseyes. I'm merely leveling the playing field."

Romeo lowered his chin and looked at her over his nose. After a moment, he nodded at the door. "We should go."

Crap. I think I embarrassed him. We used to joke about werewolves and witches all the time. What happened? "Yeah. Let's do it."

He held the screen door open for her and she waited on the porch for him to lock up. "So who are we meeting?"

They moved down the walkway toward the parked Winnebago. "His name's Bentley. He's been my mom's accountant since...well, since she got famous, I guess. But I've known him my whole life. He's the one who gave me this baby when I...well, I'd be homeless right now without him." She cleared her throat. *I know I didn't do anything wrong, but that's still humiliating to say.*

"Does he think your mom's still alive too?"

"He didn't but I think I changed his mind when I told him about the attack." They stopped on the sidewalk in front of the Winnebago, and Lily gave it a loving pat next to the door on its side. The crushed, charred dent on the other side of the door made her wince. "There's no passenger door. You can get in right here."

Romeo eyed the damaged RV, then frowned at her. "Maybe it's better if we walk."

"That offers literally no protection if another witch comes looking for me." She opened the door and gestured for him to get in.

"Right." He folded his arms. "But if another witch comes looking for you, they'll be looking for a Winnebago. Not for two people walking down the street in the middle of downtown Charleston during rush hour."

Lily's mouth dropped open for a moment before she closed the door again and frowned at the char marks on the Winnie's side. "I totally didn't think about that."

Romeo chuckled. "That's okay. We're doing this together now, so...you know. I got you. And I'm very sure I have a little more experience with lying low and slipping under someone's radar."

"Seriously?"

He rolled his eyes and shook his head. "That's a long story for another time. We can cut over to Rutledge and go down to Queen Street. We'll be there at five thirty, no problem. You uh...might wanna change your shoes, though."

Lily glanced down at her feet and felt her cheeks flush. "Oh, crap."

"Well, if a walk across town in monkey slippers is your thing..."

"No, no." She shot him an exasperated glance and smiled when he chuckled at her. "But I—" She opened the RV's side door quickly. "I was barefoot for that witch fight, and then I came here. I wasn't...uh...I grabbed the first ones I saw."

"It's a nice ice-breaker."

"Yeah, well, it wasn't supposed to be. You can come up if you want." She rolled her eyes at herself as she climbed into the Winnie to retrieve real shoes. Her cream flats were perfect, despite being a few seasons out of fashion. *And that's what happens when you lose everything of any monetary value whatsoever, isn't it?*

Romeo released a low whistle, and she turned from inside her small bedroom to see him staring at the charred bottom of the couch.

"Yeah, that's from when he missed the first time," she called and slipped her flats on.

"How many times did he miss?"

"All of them." His tense chuckle made her smile as she knelt beside the bed and took out the box of her mom's things. *Thank God they're still here.* She snatched up the glowing business card, sure to bury it in her purse so it wouldn't draw attention, and dropped the broken metal piece in after it. *I still haven't deciphered that one. But I can't take any chances.* Once she'd returned the box, she stepped out of her room and trailed her fingers along the kitchen counter. "It needs something of a remodel, probably. I would've done that if I...you know. Money doesn't buy happiness, right? But it sure can do a lot."

He smirked and studied Bentley's gift to her. "I like it."

"Well, it's home." *He can't possibly mean that.* "For now, anyway. And it's saved my skin more than a few times."

"I can see that. Are you ready?"

Lily took a deep breath. "Yeah. Let's go hide in plain sight."

When they turned onto Bull Street toward the center of downtown, she gazed at the neighborhood that looked exactly like the one they'd grown up in. "I've had next to nothing for the last two months and all this still feels like a totally different world." She studied the houses that lined the street in front of them, which would be progressively larger, more elegant, and more expensive the closer they got to Colonial Lake. On the other side of the French Quarter—where her mom had purchased a house not quite on East Bay's Rainbow Row but close enough—it was very much the same thing. "The funny thing is, I don't even remember when I stepped out of it."

"I do." Romeo's eyes sparkled but he didn't quite manage a smile.

"You mean like when my mom got famous and everyone started wanting her expertise?"

"Nope." They turned right onto Rutledge Avenue, where the houses were edged with manicured hedges and cast-iron railings instead of wooden posts bordered private yards. And there were so many more trees.

"It's when I moved to Ashley Hall for ninth grade, isn't it?" Lily traced her fingers along a waist-high wall of white stone as they passed.

"Now that was a little surprising," he said and tilted his head. "I'll give you that. You at an all-girls private school."

She shrugged. "It doesn't mean I never saw any boys in high school." He raised an eyebrow at her. "Not literally in school. After—you know what I mean." He chuckled when she nudged his arm with her elbow. *And that was solid muscle.*

"Yeah, I know you still figured out a way to have fun." He leaned away a little as if she'd been making fun of him instead. "That's what you do, isn't it?"

"Damn straight." Lily grinned at him. "I always find a good time. Even when other witches are trying to hunt me." He shot her a warning look. "Hey, I'm trying to chill and trust that if any more green fire comes out of nowhere, you can at least surprise the guy by going into wolf mode."

"Don't worry. I'm fast."

She bit her lip. "I know." They walked in silence for a minute, their faces turned into the cool ocean breeze that drifted through the hot air of the city. "So when was it, then?"

"When was what?"

She raised her hands and waved them in a big circle in front of her. "When you noticed that I'd...stepped through the portal."

Romeo took a deep breath and glanced at two pigeons

that fluttered madly across the street. One of them continued to coo when it landed on the opposite sidewalk. "That first summer when you told me you couldn't come down to Russel Creek with Dad and me. You were planning some kind of fundraiser instead."

"It's called a gala, actually." Lily smoothed a few loose strands of hair away from her face and tried to tuck them behind her ear again. "I was really upset I couldn't go but my mom wouldn't give in. It was so important to her that we used all the money she came into for...you know. Give back to the community. I don't disagree with her, right? I just... We were caught up in all kinds of social schmoozing. And I really missed you and your dad."

"Yeah, we missed you too." He looked briefly at her, then stared down the wide street again toward Colonial Lake.

FOUR

Unity Alley was exactly that—a narrow passage they entered from State Street soon after Charleston's rush-hour traffic really started to get bad. *Yeah, walking was a much better idea. If anyone attacked us now, there's no way whoever's after me could cover it up with so many witnesses.*

Once they stepped into the alley, the echo of rushing cars between so many historic buildings—much quieter on State Street than East Bay on the other side of the alley—dampened with the walls so close on either side of them now. Lily tucked her hair behind her ears and smiled at Romeo when he opened the door for her.

The alley entrance opened into the right contrast of dark, ambient setting and evening sunlight filtering through the high wall of windows around and above the door. Everything in McCrady's Tavern was stone and wood—a polished wooden bar, the flooring a mix of dark flagstone and lighter wood, wood-trimmed booths, and dark beams overhead. Soft lamps of brushed glass emitted a warm yellow glow. Opposite the long bar, brick pillars rose every few feet and combined in curving archways halfway to the ceiling that separated the restaurant into two parts—a fantastic bar on one side and better-than-fine dining on the other.

"Welcome to McCrady's Tavern," the young hostess said from behind the counter.

"Hi." Lily peered past her and caught sight of Bentley, who offered a subdued wave. "We came to meet someone."

"Sure. Go right ahead."

"Thank you." She headed past the counter with Romeo close behind her.

"Okay, you didn't tell me it was this kind of fancy. Now, I feel severely underdressed."

"Not at all." Lily gave his tight white t-shirt and dark-green Chinos shorts a quick glance. "Well, maybe. A sports jacket wouldn't hurt."

"Right. I'm fresh out of sports jackets."

"Don't worry. You look great." His eyes widened in surprise as he grinned at her. *I actually said that out loud.*

Bentley McClure sat alone, facing them, and watched them warily through his rimless silver-and-black-framed Chopard glasses. When they approached, her mom's accountant stood awkwardly from the booth and wrapped her in a huge hug. "Are you sure you're okay?" he whispered before he grabbed her by the shoulders and pushed her back to study her. "Did they hurt you?"

"Not even a little."

"Were you followed?"

Lily shook her head. "I don't think so."

"I was watching," Romeo added and nodded at Bentley. *He was?* "We didn't take the straightest route here, and I didn't see anyone follow."

Bentley glanced briefly at him, then turned toward Lily again. "This is the friend you trust?"

"Yes."

Her mom's old friend released her shoulders, scrutinized Romeo intently, and couldn't wipe the worried frown off his face. "Well, that makes you one more exception to the rule. Greta broke them all more often than not, especially as a witch with a werewolf friend of her own. So I take it you're Julian Stephens' son." The man stuck his hand out, and after a brief glance at Lily, Romeo took it.

"Romeo."

"Bentley McClure. Please, sit. I assume Lily told you what happened." The man sat back in the booth, his gaze lingering on the archway they had passed through to find his table.

They sat together on the bench opposite him. "I told him everything before I decided to call you," Lily said.

"Good. And, for all our sakes, I'd say we don't talk to anyone else about this unless we absolutely have to."

"Sure." Romeo nodded.

"Bentley, no one else believes me anyway. You didn't, either. Not that I'm complaining. You've been incredibly kind to me—"

"No, no." The man shook his head and dismissed her words with a wave. "If I had any nieces, Lily, you'd probably be more dear to me than them. I helped you because you're family. Your mom and I went way back. Or...we go way back. I actually can't believe I'm saying this, but I'm starting to see what you saw all along."

She sighed and nodded. "Thank you."

Bentley fingered the stem of his empty martini glass. "And I owe you an apology for not taking the time to listen."

Wow. He really does believe me. "Apology accepted. And I knew I could count on you."

"Always. You said Greta left you some clues."

"Right." She reached into her purse and rummaged through all the receipts and trinkets and junk she hadn't had the time to think about cleaning out. "The first thing is —hi." Lily grinned at the server who'd stopped beside their table.

"Good evening." The woman was most likely in her thirties and wore the standard black slacks with a long-sleeved white dress shirt beneath a black vest and tie. "My name's Emily, and I'll take care of you tonight. Do either of you care for a cocktail or a selection from our wine list?"

"Oh, no thank you." Lily shook her head held her hand up.

"Don't do that, Lily." Bentley nodded at her. "Order a drink. It's on me. You too, Mr. Stephens."

"Oh. Um...okay." She looked at the woman. "I'll have a glass of your rosé, please."

"Of course. And for you, sir?"

Romeo puffed out a sigh. "A...PBR's fine." Lily bit her lip and tucked her hair behind her ear.

Emily giggled, and when he didn't say anything else, her smile faded and her gaze flickered toward Lily. "Oh, I'm—I'm sorry. We don't—"

"Can you bring him whatever lager you have right now?" Lily asked.

"Sure. We have a sixteen-ounce Pinkus Mueller—"

"That's perfect. Thank you."

"Yeah, thanks," Romeo added. The woman left them to fill their drink orders, and Lily turned to Romeo with a sympathetic smile. "What kinda place doesn't have PBR?" he whispered.

"This kind of place, actually. It's okay. You'll like it." *And hopefully, he doesn't think I'm too stuck-up for knowing any of this.* "Thank you, Bentley."

The man shook his head and closed his eyes briefly. "I already ordered another martini before you arrived. If I'm drinking two because of what you told me, Lily, I can only imagine how much you'd like something to settle your own nerves. Now." He set both hands flat on the table. "I think you have something in your purse to show me."

"Right." Finally, she found the glowing purple card with "The Magic Hat" written in French. The minute she withdrew it from her purse, Bentley glanced around the restaurant quickly and pointed at the card. The glow snuffed out and the golden letters stopped changing.

"Just to be on the safe side, you understand?" The man held his hand out and she slipped the card between his fingers. He studied it for a few seconds with a frown.

"Do you know what The Magic Hat is?" Lily asked.

"It's a restaurant." Bentley looked at her. "The name is supposed to be in French. Le Chapeau Magique. Greta took many trips to Canada. This place is in Montreal, just across the US border."

"Mom never told me about it." She nodded at the card. "And it was slipped into one of our photo albums. I know she wanted me to find it but I have no idea why."

The accountant readjusted his glasses and returned the card. "It may be as simple as having to go there yourself. I'd take that card with you and see where it gets you. It has the Order of North's sigil there, so I imagine she knew it would be a safe place for you to ask questions, at the very least."

She frowned at the circle in the bottom right corner of the card. Inside it was a crescent moon with three diamonds—one in front, one behind, and one off to the side. "I didn't know they used the sigil to point sanctuaries out."

"Well, yes. Sanctuaries. Oftentimes, it's also used as a giant open sign for magicals. An invitation, if you will, to partake in whatever activity without having to hide your magic. An anything-goes type of place, I imagine."

"You've never been to one?"

"I have studied the magical societies in North America, Lily. All three of them. That is about as much excitement as I'm willing to endure when it comes to the Council and their laws."

"Fair enough."

"I'm gonna go ahead and take a wild guess on this one,"

Romeo said, "but I'm reasonably sure those orders have a list of magicals who aren't welcome."

"This is true." Bentley nodded grimly at him. "I spent quite some time...tracking your kind, Mr. Stephens. I know how to identify a werewolf as quickly as you can sniff out one of your own. Greta had a way of opening my eyes to so many misconceptions. One of those instances occurred when she introduced me to your father. I only met him once, but he's a good man." He sighed and looked at the card in Lily's hand again. "That said, if you weren't Lily's friend, I'd tell you to stay as far away from Le Chapeau Magique as you can. But under the circumstances, I think you could get by with being her guest. If that's where you decide you want to go, of course."

"Thanks." Romeo's brows lifted in uncertainty. "I think."

Lily looked at the card once more. *I bet Romeo will want to have another conversation about this later. I had no idea Bentley and Julian ever met.* "What about this?" She pointed to the black silhouette of a bird in flight on the bottom corner of the card. "What is that? A crane?"

"Not a crane." Romeo leaned toward her to look over her shoulder. His arm brushed against her, and she dared herself to look at him when he was this close. "That's a heron."

She squinted at the silhouette. "Are you sure?"

"Oh, yeah. If you know what to look for, there's a big difference. With cranes and herons, it's mostly the neck. Cranes don't bend theirs like that when they fly."

Lily smiled at him and her gaze drifted to his lips. "I didn't know you were big into bird-watching."

He glanced at Bentley, then back at her. "I wouldn't say big into it. There's nothing wrong with sitting on a dock to watch a few birds." He grinned at her, and when Bentley cleared his throat, the moment was broken.

"Any idea what the black heron means?" she asked the older man and wished her heart would stop the odd flutter it had developed.

"I couldn't say. It's not a sigil for any order I know so it may only be a bird on a business card." He looked up when the server returned to their table with a tray and three drinks.

"For you, Mr. McClure," she said and set down a second, almost overflowing martini glass.

He handed her the empty glass. "Thank you."

"The Lorenza Rosé...and the Pinkus."

Romeo didn't look up from the card in Lily's hand.

"Thanks so much." She smiled at the server, took both drinks, and set them down in front of them.

"Is there anything else I can get for you?"

"Not right now, Emily. Thank you." Bentley nodded at Lily, who raised her wineglass in a wordless toast. *I don't know what I'd do if he didn't believe me right now.*

"Of course." The woman tucked the tray under her arm and left.

"Okay, so we covered the business card." Lily tapped it, then looked through her purse again. "But I found this too." She retrieved the broken piece of metal from her purse and set it on the table. "I have absolutely no idea what it is. But I know Mom hid it in all the stuff she knew I'd want to keep." *Exactly like she knew basically every-thing I'd do before I did it.*

"Can I take a look?" Romeo held his hand out, and she dropped the broken chunk of whatever it was quickly into his open palm. He turned it over between his fingers. "It kinda looks like a pair of wings...but I'm not sure what would've been attached to it. Maybe flames?"

"Well, if that's what it is, we still haven't narrowed down the options," Lily responded.

"What about those?" He placed the broken piece of wings or flames on the table and pointed to the barely visible lettering stamped sideways across the fragment in the same direction as the pieces that looked like wings.

"L-A-N-T," Lily muttered, then looked at Bentley. "Does that mean anything to you?"

The accountant shook his head and pushed his glasses up. "It doesn't. Knowing your mother, all I can say is that looks an awful lot like an invitation to find the other piece."

"Yeah, that's what I thought. Except that's hard to do when I have no idea where to find it." She looked at the older man again, and his raised eyebrows over a small, nostalgic smile turned the lightbulb on in her head. "Or she's saying I have to find the other piece at Le Chapeau Magique."

Bentley took a long sip of his martini. "That's what I would suggest."

"Hey, Romeo?" When he looked at her, she wiggled her eyebrows. "How do you feel about a road trip to Canada?"

He licked his lips. "Well, I've never been there either. It sounds perfect."

And he's worried about being a werewolf in a restaurant welcoming all magicals except werewolves. I can't blame him for that. "Don't worry." She nudged his ribs with her elbow. "I got you. And I'm fairly certain I have a little more experience walking into a place full of witches."

He snorted and shook his head but couldn't hide the smile when he looked at his lap. Finally, he picked his beer glass up for the first time and drained most of it in a few seconds.

"I guess that's it, then, right? We'll go to Montreal." With a shrug, she stuck the card and the broken piece of metal in her purse and patted Romeo's arm.

"Ready when you are." It took a moment before he looked at her and realized she was waiting for him to get out of the booth. "Right." He slid out and she followed.

"Wait a minute." Bentley slithered out of his booth too and spread his arms. "If you're following whatever trail Greta left for you, I imagine I won't see you for some time. But it's better to know that you won't be alone." He nodded at Romeo, who looked surprised but nodded in response. Lily stepped into the man's embrace and squeezed him tightly. "Do you need any money?" he whispered.

"No. You've given me more than enough."

He patted her back. "It wasn't that much." When he released her, she wanted to hug him again. *But we have to keep going.*

"I've actually been really careful with it." She chuckled. "I'm glad you listened to what I had to say. It's been—"

"Tough. I know." Bentley smoothed the hair back from her forehead. "Your mother always believed in you. If you're right, Lily, she still does. I think it's the best choice for you to follow what she left you. And mostly to get out of Charleston before the next witch takes a shot at you."

"They can try." She grinned.

"You are so much like her. Okay. Get going." He looked past her to meet Romeo's gaze. "Mr. Stephens, I hope you know how important it is to keep her safe."

Romeo's eyes widened before he shook his head. "Lily doesn't need anyone to keep her safe. I'm merely her sidekick."

Bentley tilted his head and smiled despite his own fear of what Lily would find on this adventure of hers. He raised a hand to wave goodbye as they turned and walked away.

The mugginess of Charleston's evening air struck her in a wave when she stepped outside. For a minute, she simply stood at the entrance to McCrady's Tavern, drew deep breaths, and smoothed the hair away from her face.

"Are you okay?" Romeo slipped through the door and the two of them stepped across Unity Alley to make room for a small group who entered the restaurant.

"Yeah." Lily blinked fiercely and shook her head. "I think so. I had no idea Bentley knew your dad."

"It's a little weird, admittedly. I'd say it was a plus, though. The guy seems to think I'm okay."

She bumped him with her shoulder. "You're more than

okay. Look, about the whole werewolves not being welcome around other magicals—"

"Don't sweat it. I know it's not about me personally."

Lily looked at him and tilted her chin. "It shouldn't be a law in the first place. I know it's stupid and you're not dangerous to anybody."

"Only if they get in my way." He shrugged, his expression stern. "Or try to hurt you."

He's coming on strong with that one, isn't he? Yes, I like it. "You said I didn't need protection."

"You don't." They retraced their steps down the alley toward State Street. "It doesn't mean I'm gonna sit and do nothing if you're in trouble."

"Well, that's very chivalrous of you." She winked at him and they turned into downtown Charleston's open sea air. The city was lively with the sounds of people ending the day with good food and great drinks and the kicking nightlife every day of the week.

"Do you think it's safe to stick around any longer tonight?" Romeo asked. "We could leave early in the morning."

"I really don't know. It's not like I'm heading to Canada to run away from whoever thinks I'm a loose end. I can take 'em—well, as long as it's not a whole coven at the same time." Romeo smirked at her. "Why?"

"Well, I can think of one person who'd really like to see you tonight."

"You're talking about your dad, aren't you?" Lily adjusted the strap of her purse and tried not to look turned off by the idea.

"Good guess."

"I dunno, Romeo..." *That feels too much like stepping into the past. He probably won't even recognize me.*

"Oh, come on. Why not?"

"Honestly?"

"Yeah." He shoved his hands in his pockets and smiled at her with his mouth open and his eyes crinkled, on the verge of laughter.

"Okay, that year I stopped going down to Edisto with you guys...I forgot to call him on his birthday."

He laughed for real. "What?"

"Yeah, I know. It's not that big a deal, but I was mortified. You can bet I remembered it the next year, but at that point, I was convinced he was angry at me. So I kept beating myself up every year."

Romeo chuckled. "You were totally wrong. He'd never hold that against you."

"I know...I was also twelve. I set myself up for that one." She shook her head. "Are you sure he wants to see me?"

"Let's put it this way. If he finds out you stopped by and I never told him, he won't let me forget it for the next five years, at least." He looked at her, took a deep breath, and nodded. "So yes, it's great to have a little reunion. Mostly, I try to keep the old man fat and happy. It makes my life a whole lot easier." He was only half-joking, but her wide-eyed disbelief made him crack up. "By the way, I know the first thing we'll do when we hit the road to Canada."

"Oh, really?"

"I'll buy us a six-pack of PBR, and you're gonna drink it with me."

Lily made a face. "You'll have to tie me down and feed it to me through a tube if you're gonna be successful."

He grinned. "Hey, I have no problem with tying you down."

"Yeah, I bet you don't."

FIVE

When they finally ended their half-hour walk back to Romeo's house, Lily's stomach was growling virtually every two minutes.

They stopped beside her Winnebago, and she stared at the house Romeo shared with his dad. "Maybe it's better if I take the Winnie and go. I know my life's kinda dangerous right now, but I don't know how dangerous. You guys don't deserve to be pulled into this."

"Well, so far, you haven't been attacked by any asshole witches since you showed up at my door. They might not even wanna touch you with a werewolf around. Or two." Romeo nodded at the front door.

"It's not impossible." She put a hand on her hip. "But it's more likely that I threw them off the trail when the last guy lost consciousness and his memory. At least for a while."

"Yeah, it's not impossible."

"I guess it would be kinda awkward, though, if I sat in

the Winnie all night and never came in." She bit her lip and scowled at the charred dent in the side of her RV. "It would be totally stupid to go back to that garage."

"Why would you go back?"

"Uh...that's where I've kept this thing. On Meeting Street."

Romeo pressed his lips together and ran a hand through his hair. "Is that... I mean, is it legal?"

"Yeah, actually. They have RV parking, and it's surprisingly cheap. I didn't think it would be an open invitation for someone to murder me."

He tried to hold back a smile but failed. "You've been boondocking on Meeting Street."

Lily smirked and shoved him gently in the chest. "Not my proudest moment, okay? It was better than Tent City. And it's not boondocking if I pay for it. From what I've heard, independent parking is the preferred phrase."

"Look at that. You learn something new every day."

"Do you think your dad will mind if I keep it here tonight before we leave?"

Romeo's eyes sparkled and he gave her his careless half smile. "It's my house too, you know."

"Okay. Do you mind?"

He took a few seconds longer to answer, simply because he liked how she looked at him when she wanted something. "No. I want you to stay."

Lily swallowed and lowered her head. "Well, thanks. I mean it, though. If any more witches show up looking for a fight they think they can handle, I'll get as far away from your house as I possibly can."

"Noted. Canada's fairly far. But don't leave without me."

She closed her eyes with a little laugh, and the screen door opened with a squeak and closed with a bang.

"Lily?" Julian Stephens walked briskly down the driveway. He grinned at her as he wiped his hands on a yellow dishrag. "Well, I'll be damned. Is that Miss Lily Antony standing in front of my house?"

"Hi." Lily raised her hand in a quick wave, then leaned toward Romeo. "You said you were keeping him fat and happy."

"What? That's only an expression."

Romeo's dad had the same black hair, only he kept his short above a neatly trimmed beard and mustache. His eyes were brown rather than Romeo's green, and when he stopped at the edge of the sidewalk, Lily noticed the new wrinkle lines at the corners of his eyes and around his mouth. Other than that, he was exactly as she remembered him.

"Ain't this somethin'?" Julian glanced from one to the other for a few seconds as if looking for something else to say before he took a deep breath. "Look at you. I haven't seen you in...longer'n I care to think about. Come here." He almost leapt off the sidewalk to wrap her in a tight, rather sweaty hug. Romeo chuckled and her eyes widened as she patted his back gently.

Finally, he released her, then grabbed her by both shoulders and studied her. "My God. You're the spittin' image of your mama." His grin faded, and his dark brows drew together in a frown. "Lily, I am so sorry for your loss."

She swallowed. "Thank you."

"How you holdin' up?"

She glanced at Romeo, who chewed on the inside of his cheek again. "I'm...okay. Trying to move through it, you know?"

"Sure, sure." Julian nodded, then glanced at his son and perked up again. "Tell ya what. I'm fixin' to put supper on. Are you hungry?"

"Uh, well—"

"Oh. Oh, I'm sorry. Were y'all in the middle of a chat?" He flicked the dishrag between them. "That's fine. Finish up, then come on inside. I put the water on for a crab boil, so y'all got some time." The man nodded, grinned at Lily again, and slung the rag over his shoulder and walked up the driveway.

Once the screen door slammed shut on the porch, she puffed out a sigh. "Wow."

Romeo snorted. "Yep. He's...still Dad."

She turned to look at him with wide eyes. "He is so Southern."

"Well, yeah. We all are."

"No, I mean...did he always talk like that?"

"Mm-hmm."

"But you don't."

He opened his mouth, shut it, and tipped his head back to look down his nose at her. "He spends a lot more time down in Edisto than I do. I guess I grew out of it. Of course, I didn't go to Ashley Hall or anything."

Lily shook her head. "I don't think that has anything to do with it."

Laughing, he stepped toward her and placed his hand on the small of her back to guide her up the driveway. "It's like old times, right? You look like you could use some of that right about now."

She let him usher her to the front door. *It's only a friendly hand on my back. From a very friendly...friend.* "Yeah, but I didn't quite expect the Julian Special."

Romeo cocked his head and grinned. "It's a package deal, babe. If you want this sidekick, you gotta sit down and eat that man's cookin'."

"Wow, you're offering a package deal, huh?" Her stomach fluttered when his hand left her back to hold the door open for her.

"Yes, ma'am. I reckon I am."

They were both laughing when they stepped inside, and Lily waited for him to close the front door behind them. She'd had any number of gourmet meals since they had actually been an option for her and her mom, but there was nothing like the smell of Old Bay boiling in someone's kitchen. Steam rose in billowing clouds from the huge pot on the stove, where Julian lowered blue crabs into the scalding water.

"Oh, jeeze," she whispered.

"Are you okay?" Romeo leaned forward to look at her. "You look a little pale."

"They're still moving." She grimaced at the wriggling crab before Julian dropped it in the pot, then glanced at the ceiling.

"Don't tell me you forgot how it's done."

"Maybe a little." She shrugged and smiled at him. "It's been a while since I watched anyone cook like this."

"Well, welcome back to your childhood." Chuckling, Romeo headed past her to the fridge. As soon as he grabbed the handle, he paused.

He sees the picture. She shifted her weight and watched him, but he didn't look at her and he didn't mention a thing before he opened the door and looked inside.

"Yeah, whatever suits y'all," Julian called from the stove. "We got a few cokes. Maybe a beer or two. Should still be some sweet tea in there."

Romeo turned back from the fridge and grinned at Lily as he tipped a cold can of PBR back and forth.

"I'll have some sweet tea, thanks," she said and made a face at him.

"Sure. Glasses are in the cupboard." Julian nodded toward the cabinets beside the fridge.

She retrieved three glasses and tried not to laugh at the exaggerated show Romeo made of popping the beer can open and guzzling the first gulp. He sighed and smacked his lips, then grabbed the pitcher of sweet tea from the fridge and headed toward the table. She helped him set their places with plates, forks, crab forks, and napkins.

"Don't forget that summer salad," Julian called and pointed a pair of tongs at them. "I made that this mornin'."

"Hey, I do have one small favor," Romeo whispered over the table as they set it.

"Go for it."

"Can we not tell him exactly what's going on right

now? He's going through some stuff. I don't know if he could handle thinking that your mom's...missing instead."

"My lips are sealed." She mimed zipping her lips closed and tossing the key away. "Feel free to come up with a good cover."

SIX

By the time Julian took half a bushel of steamed blue crabs out of the pot and set them on a serving dish, the table was fully set—including the shallow dishes of melted butter—and Lily had gone through a glass and a half of sweet tea. *I don't think I've had this much sugar without alcohol in it for years.* She smiled at Julian when she passed him to dilute the rest of her drink with tap water. Then, she joined the two men at the table, scooted herself in, and gazed at the relatively simple meal in front of her. It smelled amazing.

The older man grabbed his napkin, shook it open, and tucked it into the collar of his shirt. Lily spread hers out on her lap, and Romeo snorted. "What?"

"You're gettin' fancy," he said.

"Lily can be as fancy as she wants to here," Julian said and plopped two crispy blue crabs on his plate before he slung a huge one onto hers. "So long as she doesn't expect it from us." He winked at her and passed his son the salad bowl. "So go 'head and spill it, Lily. What you been up to since I saw you last?" His crab fork clinked onto his plate when he slammed his elbow down on the table and smiled at her with wide eyes. "I can't believe it's been so long."

"I know. I'm sorry about that." She picked at the crab with her fingertips to find the best place to break it open.

"Naw, naw. I ain't lookin' for an apology. I'm happy to see ya."

"Well, you know Mom and I were living right behind East Bay, right?"

His eyes widened and he uttered a small exclamation of surprise around a mouthful of crabmeat. "Yeah, that's a nice area." He swallowed and frowned. "You're not there anymore?"

Romeo pressed his lips together, punctuated by the harsh crack as his crab fork ripped through the softer underbelly of his dinner.

"No, not anymore. I, uh...I kind of lost everything when she was declared dead. It was unexpected, so I'm trying to get back on my feet now."

Romeo glanced at her with wide eyes and crammed a chunk of crabmeat dripping with butter into his mouth.

"Oh. Well, you could've come here, Lily. Taken Romeo's room. Hell, I'd have given you mine."

Lily chuckled. "That's a...kind gesture, Julian. I actually think I like being on my own a little better. That way, I don't bother anyone." *Or put them in danger, apparently.*

"Sure, sure. Everyone's got their own way of livin'. Where's home for you these days?"

"That RV outside." She forced back a laugh when he made a long, exaggerated face of surprise.

"Yeah, that's a nice big model. Plenty of space." He tipped his fork toward his son. "Didn't your Aunt Helen have one of them in Beaufort?"

"Probably." Romeo cracked open the crab shell even more.

"Yeah, it was actually a gift. From Bentley McClure. I heard you met him once."

"Hmm. Yeah. Fine man, once he got over your mama and me breaking all kindsa magic rules just bein' friends. Never understood that superior thinkin'."

"It doesn't make sense to me, either." All but stabbing at her crab now with the fork, Lily gave up. The fork dropped to her plate and she spread her fingers along the crab to break it open with her magic.

"Would you look at that." Julian's eyes widened again, and he smothered a guffaw. "That how you witches set to crackin' dinner open around those high-society folks?" Romeo snorted again and his dad chuckled, his hazel eyes glinting at Lily under the kitchen lights. He stuck another piece of buttery crabmeat into his mouth.

"Only when the crab forks are as old and dull as yours." She pursed her lips and tried to hide her own smile.

The older man topped her drink off with the pitcher of sweet tea. "You know, if you wanted to get me a birthday present to make up for all those missed phone calls..."

Lily jerked forward to keep her food in her mouth, then stared at Romeo. "You said he wouldn't hold it against me."

Julian chuckled and tapped his fork on the table beside her plate. "I'm only pullin' your leg, darlin'. I know you and Greta had a lot goin' on once she made it up there to the top of the ladder. And I don't expect any gifts from you until you're back on your feet."

"Well..." Lily and Romeo shared a quick glance. "I'm working on it."

He nodded slowly, his gaze now focused entirely on his second crab beside the picked-clean shell of the first. "I can only imagine," he said. "Your mama and me, Lily...well, we helped each other through some hard times back in the day, didn't we?" She glanced at Romeo, who finished his second crab before he tossed the shells and selected a third. "Helped you young'uns too, huh? Everybody needs a friend, especially when the going gets tough."

Her cheeks flushed hot. "Yeah, I can agree with that." Romeo glanced at her and winked. She grinned and clenched her eyes shut when melted butter dribbled down his chin.

"Oh—jeeze." He leaned over his plate and tried to wipe it off.

"You goin' to school?" Julian asked and sucked the butter off his fingers.

"No. I, uh...college didn't feel right after high school. I preferred what Mom was teaching me anyway, so I opted to go with that."

"No kiddin'? Romeo said basically the same thing after he graduated. Never went to college, either."

Romeo dropped his own crab onto his plate with a thunk and spread his hands. "Dad—"

"Oh, come on. It's the truth. Ain't no shame in tellin' what's true. Besides, we've always had our own ways of makin' do with what we got." Julian nodded and winked at Lily again, then returned to his food.

She tried to distract herself by serving a portion of the man's summer salad onto her plate—spinach leaves, strawberries, goat cheese, onions, pine nuts, and what she guessed was balsamic vinaigrette. A quick glance at Romeo from the corner of her eye revealed him remarkably focused on splitting a crab leg he'd already emptied.

"So. Not that I'm complaining, Lily, because I am not. It's a joy to see you again. Especially in this house. But I can't help but wonder what brought you back here, right outta the blue." Julian smiled at her, his forearms resting on the table as he picked at his crab over his plate.

"You picked up on that, huh?" She smiled and shrugged. "Like you said. Everybody needs a friend." More heat rose in her cheeks, but she went ahead and said the next part anyway. "Romeo's basically the only friend I have right now." A small, choked-up giggle escaped her.

Julian looked from her to his son and back at her again. "Well, ain't that somethin'. Whatcha need him for?"

"Dad, you know Lily doesn't need anybody for anything." Romeo glanced at her, and both he and his dad chuckled a little.

"Oh, I know. I knew since you were a little miss runnin' around, tellin' the world to 'Watch out!' I only meant what y'all have planned. 'Cause y'all look like yer plannin' somethin'."

"We're going camping," Romeo said and sounded a

little too enthusiastic as he snatched up his glass of sweet tea. Lily turned slowly to him and widened her eyes. He nodded at her, lifted his glass, and took a long sip.

"Camping, huh? Where at?"

"Um...up north," she said. Romeo snorted and almost sprayed sweet tea through his nose. She fought to keep from laughing.

"Hmm." Julian crammed a huge forkful of salad into his mouth. "Well if it's way north, y'all make sure to show those Yanks how it's done down here."

"You got it," his son said and shook his head.

"Camping." The older man tossed his second empty crab into the shell bowl, plucked another from the platter, and held it over his plate while he leaned back in his chair. "I remember..." He chuckled, then he had to fight through his laughter to keep speaking. "I remember when the four of us went down to Edisto one summer. Took our tents and sleeping bags 'cause my cousin's cabin on Russel Creek had all that flood damage from the hurricane."

"Oh, no..." Lily covered her face with a hand.

"Y'all remember that?"

"About the bears?" Romeo said and he started laughing too.

"The two...the two of y'all were talkin' about bears all day while we set up." Julian gasped for breath through his laughter. "Wanted to try to...try to catch you one. Then at night, Lily snuck outta her mama's tent—"

"I was hungry, okay?" She spread her hands and leaned over the table. "That was a stupid rule not to let us eat after dark, by the way."

Julian bellowed with laughter. "That was all we had for the next day. And you laid it all out on the picnic table and made yourself a little feast."

"I thought Dad was gonna have a heart attack when you fell into our tent," Romeo added, laughing now too. "'The bears! The bears found us. Run for your lives!'"

"It was a raccoon!" Julian hooted and slapped the table.

"Two!" Lily shouted in response as she leaned forward and waved two fingers in Julian's face. "Two racoons, okay? And they might as well have been bears. They were huge." Both men laughed even harder at that, and she simply shook her head. "Yeah, yeah. Laugh it up. Don't tell me you wouldn't have been freaked out as a nine-year-old if you found two giant rats falling out of the trees to steal your food."

"Rats?" Julian howled with laughter.

"You let them take it all," Romeo added. "We had to drive all the way back to King's Market so we could eat the next morning."

"Oh, right. And you would've chased them off, huh?" She tilted her chin at him in a challenge but failed to look serious.

Romeo's smile faded a little as he held her gaze. "I have," he said. Then he swallowed and looked at his dad with another chuckle. "I'd say I've gotten good at chasing racoons off. And rats." Julian barked out a laugh. "Two totally different things, Lily, by the way."

"Yeah, I know that now." Grinning, she took a long drink of her watered-down sweet tea.

"Oh, and your mama had to pull a little magic trick with that one," Julian added.

"Very funny," she said.

"She only summoned a little...I dunno...gate or something so those animals couldn't get back into our food." He wiggled his fingers at her. "She sat there cookin' us breakfast and shakin' her head at you."

"Yeah, she cast a barrier spell around the cooler," Lily said, "but she made me put your tent up without any magic at all."

"And she made me help," Romeo added.

"Aw, it was good for you." Julian waved a hand at them and sat in his chair again as he wiped the tears from his eyes. "Yeah, she was medicine for all of us. Took me too long to realize how good we had it, even back then." He sniffed, gave a little shrug, then folded his arms. "I miss the days where a fake bear was the worst of our problems." The kitchen seemed suddenly quiet, then, broken only by a few more chuckles spilling out of Romeo's dad as he went through his own memories again in private. "I miss your mama, Lily. I really do."

She took a deep breath and slowly released it. "Me too."

"Well." The older man leaned over his plate and directed his attention to his attempt to open another crab. "Ain't nothin' more important than family. Your mama always said that, and I've always felt the same. You're family to us too, Lily. Don't forget that. No matter how long it takes you to find your way back home."

Lily smiled but couldn't look the man in the eye. *Let's*

keep the waterworks back, huh? Instead, she reached out to grab another crab from the platter and didn't even try to break it open with a fork this time.

"The two of y'all are gonna have a big time goin' out together. Campin'." He chuckled and shook his head, then waved his crab fork a few times at Lily and Romeo. "It's good to see y'all headin' off together on another adventure. And takin' care of each other."

She pried open her magically cracked dinner and slipped a huge piece of crabmeat into the butter dish. Romeo elbowed her in the side. "Don't worry," he said with a smirk. "You take care of the spells. I'll handle the bears. And the raccoons."

They sat around the table for a long time after dinner, talking and swapping stories. Most of them had to do with Lily's mom in one way or another, and they couldn't really avoid bringing up the attempted witch fry in the parking garage if they only talked about Lily.

Finally, Julian stretched his arms high above his head and uttered a massive yawn that sounded more like a growl. "Well, now. This old dog needs to go lie down." She glanced at Romeo, who smiled a little, closed his eyes, and shook his head.

"We'll wash up," he told his dad.

" 'Preciate it. Night, Lily. If I don't see you before y'all leave, I'm so glad you decided to drop by."

She stood and allowed him to almost crush her in another of his massive hugs. "Thanks for dinner," she said. "It's good to be back here after so long."

"That it is." He released her, grabbed her upper arms,

and gave them a little squeeze. "That it is. Y'all enjoy your-selves, then. Have a good night." Julian nodded at them both and shuffled toward the back of the house and his bedroom.

"Time to scrub some dishes," Romeo said and wiggled his eyebrows.

"That's always my favorite part of having someone else cook for me."

"See, I can tell you're lying." He stood from the table, and Lily helped him gather the plates and scrape all the crab shells into the trash. At the sink, he rinsed the dishes off with a sponge before he handed them to her to put in the dishwasher.

"Massive *déjà vu*, right?"

Romeo raised an eyebrow. "Fond memories of our indentured servitude as kids, huh?"

"Oh, it wasn't that bad. How's he really doing? Your dad."

He shrugged and handed her a dripping plate. "He's been better. Been worse too, so I don't really know. I think he's lonely, mostly. A few of his friends passed in the last couple months."

"Were they close?"

He looked at her and raised an eyebrow. "I mean, they were wolf friends, so yeah, they were close. I'm not sure Dad's ever really been part of a pack, strictly speaking, but I think it was almost the same thing."

"I'm sorry." Lily swiped the hair away from her fore-head with the back of her forearm and put two more cups on the rack. "Are you?"

Romeo chuckled. "Am I what?"

"Part of a pack?"

He lowered his hands into the sink and turned to look at her. "Nope. My options are a little...limited. At least here." His green eyes bored into hers, then he took a quick breath and went back to the dishes. "I never said I didn't have any selfish reasons for coming on this trip with you. I want to come with you, don't get me wrong. Even if you don't need me."

She bit her lip and watched him scrub furiously at a plate he'd already rinsed fairly clean.

"You just...gave me the perfect opportunity to get outta here too, you know? That's been hard for me."

"Yeah, that's a good reason. And I'm totally okay with that."

When they finished, they dried their hands off and Romeo started the dishwasher. He wiped his hands on his shorts and sighed as he glanced around the dark, quiet house where he still lived with his dad. "You know, I'd offer you a place to sleep, but..." He laughed. "It looks like you don't really need one."

"Hey, what a funny joke. You're right, though. I have everything I need back there in that beautiful box on wheels. Hey, can I use your shower first?"

He squinted at her. "The box on wheels didn't come with a shower?"

"No, it definitely has one. It...uh, it's got a few problems, and I haven't been able to find out how to fix it."

"We should probably take a look at that before we hit the road, right?"

Lily sighed. "It works but not the way I want."

"What?"

"Hey, don't laugh at me. I'll tell you about it later. Can I please use your shower?"

Romeo studied her for a few seconds and his smile broadened. "Yeah. Lemme get you a towel."

She'd told him she wouldn't take very long, but when she stepped under the hot water, she realized she could actually stay there for longer than four and a half minutes. Having timed more showers in the Winnebago than she could count, the overwhelming temptation to linger until the hot water ran out won the debate.

"Boy, wiping a stranger's memory really takes it out of you," she whispered when she stepped out onto the bath-mat. It took her a few more minutes to dry herself and finger-brush her hair enough that it didn't look so soaked and messy. Unfortunately, she had to pull her slightly sweaty clothes on, although she picked her flats up to carry them with her.

"Thank you so much, Romeo," she said when she stepped back into the living room. "That was a life—"

A deep, gurgling snore cut her off. He sprawled out on the couch—the same couch she'd sat on that afternoon to talk with him for the first time in seven years. He'd passed out completely with one hand on his chest. The other dangled off the side of the couch and his knuckles almost brushed the rug. She watched him for a few more seconds, then let herself out the front door to climb into the Winnebago and what had become her home over the last two months.

When she flopped onto the queen-sized bed in the back of the RV, Lily spread her arms across the comforter and stared at the ceiling. "Okay, Mom. I found your clues. Hang on a little longer. I'm coming."

THE SHADOW of a huge black bird rippled over the darkened street toward Ashley Avenue and descended slowly. When it found the Winnebago Adventurer pulled up to the curb, it drifted onto the RVs roof, through the metal, and hovered in the air above Lily's sleeping form. *Time is running out.* The words were barely loud enough to enter her dreams before the shadow slipped into a thin, slithering line and disappeared into the young witch's open mouth.

SEVEN

Someone knocked on the Winnebago and Lily groaned, rolled over in bed, and jammed her pillow over her head. The knock came again, a little louder this time. After a third strong rap, She whipped the pillow off her face and yelled in her loudest, barely-out-of-sleep voice, "It's open!"

"Well, yeah. I worked that part out."

"What the—" Surprised into defense mode, Lily jolted up from where she lay and released a minor disarming spell at the dark, blurry figure that hovered in the narrow doorway to her bedroom.

"Woah!" The man ducked, and the red-sparking spell that streaked from her outstretched fingers did nothing more than leave a charred black mark on the corner of her built-in wardrobe. Romeo's laughter filled the RV, joined by the smell of singed wood. "You know, I think your aim might be at its best when you're half asleep. You almost got me."

"Romeo?" she gasped and scrambled to pull the sheets over herself now that she could see and think again.

"You sleep naked, huh?"

"I—what? You just... That's the worst wakeup call ever. What are you doing here?"

"You said it was open."

"Yeah, that was after you already—" She huffed in frustration and relief around the grogginess that hadn't quite cleared. Her scowl deepened as she smoothed the mess of her hair away from her face with one hand while holding the sheets up to her neck with the other. "What time is it?"

He leaned against the doorway and folded his arms. "Seven."

"In the morning?"

"You know, I'm tempted to see if you really could sleep until seven at night, but I thought we wanted to get a head start on this road trip. Right?"

"Yeah, but..." Lily blinked away the double image of Romeo smirking at her until she glared at only one of him. "Seven o'clock in the morning?"

"It's really not that early," he said. "We might be able to beat rush-hour traffic on I-26 if we leave in like...ten minutes."

A huge yawn split her jaws wide. "Okay. Yeah. You're right. Do you know how far we have to drive?"

"About eighteen hours if we went straight through. Probably a few hours extra for...you know. Stopping to fill up and everything." He patted the wall beside him and grinned.

Lily closed her eyes and exhaled a long sigh. "Thanks

for getting me up. I'll be out in a minute." He merely stared at her. "After I get some clothes on, huh?"

Romeo studied her for a few seconds. "Sure. No problem." He nodded and turned toward the front of the RV. "I'll be in the house. When you're ready to get moving."

"Romeo?" He turned to look at her with wide eyes, and she licked her lips and didn't quite manage to clear away her own smirk when she tilted her head at him. "What did you see?"

He shook his head, lowered his gaze, and scratched behind his ear. "Nothing." He started to leave and paused, unable to make up his mind, then shook his head again and smiled at the Winnie's carpeted floors. "Nothing." The RV rocked a little as he made his way through the narrow back hallway and out toward the main living space which was actually fairly roomy as far as RVs went.

When she heard the front door close behind him, Lily released the breath she'd been holding and laughed at herself. "Yes, I sleep naked. At least he covered one of those ground rules." She tossed the sheets aside, and her gaze fell on the charred wood of the hinged closet door with the mirror mounted in the center. "I could have taken his hand off with that spell. Maybe I do have better aim when I'm half asleep." She scoffed, stood, and took the two steps across the small room between her bed and the wardrobe.

Her collection of clothing and accessories wasn't lacking at first glance, although it was only about a fifth of what she'd had before the fake will had taken everything she actually liked. "I don't have much road-trip garb. Okay, what do we have?" She rummaged through the drawers and found her faded yellow Lululemon jogger capris. Lily tossed them aside, hoping to find something better. "Tennis skirt? Nope. I'm literally gonna be sitting all day. Where are those—"

She grunted in frustration and flopped her hands against her thighs. "Calm down, Lily. Your clothes are definitely not what make you capable of doing this. You know that. Romeo wouldn't care if you wore a bathing suit all day. No, actually. He'd probably like that." Snorting, she swiped hastily through the clothes hanging on the short metal bar and folded semi-neatly into the ten drawers stacked below the wardrobe. Chewing on her fingernail, she turned and studied the capris. "Lululemon it is, then." She snatched a thin-strap tank top with stripes of white and various shades of blue, tugged it over her head, and slipped into the cropped leggings.

When she looked at her reflection in the wardrobe's mirror, she shook her head and moved to the bathroom. "Why am I freaking out about what to wear in an RV all day?" She snatched her hairbrush from the built-in cubby so hard, it almost slipped out of her hand again. "You're friends. He's coming because he wants to. You would've done this anyway without him and not worried at all about what you wore, so stop." She brushed her blonde hair furiously and continued to lecture her reflection in the mirror above the sink. "This is real. Mom's still alive. Keep your eyes open, look at things the way Mom taught you, and don't give up. That's the most important—" She smacked her lips a few times and ran her tongue along the roof of her mouth. "I have never tasted that before. Even first thing in the morning." Her next glance at the mirror made her freeze.

A black shadow with outstretched wings hovered behind her.

Lily whirled to face it and had already begun to summon an attack, but there was nothing there. It was gone from her reflection too.

She tied her hair back to brush her teeth and managed to mostly eradicate the weird, smoky taste. Out into the living area, she muttered in irritation before she darted back into the bathroom to put deodorant on. As she climbed down out of the RV, she paused and frowned. "Should I look for that shadow? I mean—no. It must have been a trick of the light, and if it wanted to kill me, it had the perfect chance." She took a deep breath, rolled her shoulders back, and closed the Winnebago door.

"'Morning, Lily."

"Oh, my—jeeze." She stumbled over her first step onto the sidewalk and looked up.

Romeo and Julian sat on the front porch, each of them with a plate on their laps. The older man lifted his fork in greeting.

"'Morning," she said and moved up the walkway toward them. "How long have you sat there watching me?" When she reached the porch, they were both still staring at her with broad smiles appearing between mouthfuls.

"Only once you stepped out. Are you okay?" Romeo asked and held her gaze over the rim of his coffee cup as he took a sip.

"Yeah. I'm fine. Just..." She brushed her hair aside and glanced at the Winnie. "I thought I saw something but I'm still trying to wake up."

"Something I should know about?" he asked and referred to the death price some witch had put on her head.

"I don't think so."

"You were makin' an awful lotta noise in there," Julian said. If he'd tried not to laugh, a chuckle escaped anyway.

"Well..." Lily cocked her head at Romeo and smirked. "Somebody startled me awake. Maybe I'm a little jumpy."

"Sorry. I didn't think about it like that." He laughed and leaned away from her when she reached down to grab the coffee mug out of his hand.

"Apology accepted. Thank you for the coffee."

"Hey—" He didn't actually resist and his father chuckled.

She took a few sips of perfectly warm coffee, lifted the mug with both hands, and raised her eyebrows. "This, Romeo. This is how you wake a girl up in the morning."

"Woo." Grinning, Julian shook his head and scooped another forkful of food into his mouth.

"Are there any eggs left?" she asked.

"And bacon." Romeo wiggled his eyebrows.

"Perfect." She shot him a pert smile, opened the screen door, and headed inside to the kitchen, taking his coffee with her.

The bacon smelled like heaven. *Greasy, fattening, straight-to-my-hips heaven.* Lily nodded firmly and pulled a plate out of the cupboard. Only the low drone of the men's voices out on the porch disturbed the silence. Once she'd served herself a plate of eggs from the still-warm pan on the stove—plus an extra helping or two of crispy bacon from the grease-soaked paper towel—she took her plate to the table and dug in. Romeo chose that moment to follow her inside.

By the time he'd tossed a few more bacon strips on his own plate and came to join her at the table, she'd eaten half her food. The crunch of the best part of all pigs every-where filled the kitchen, and Lily leaned back with a contented sigh.

Romeo laughed. "Okay...so now that we've tamed the beast—"

"Hey." She pointed at him and spoke around a mouthful of heaven. "Doesn't that phrase only apply to you?"

"Not if you don't want it to."

She raised an eyebrow and turned her head a little. "I'll think about it. Hey, did you see anything...weird this morning?"

"Besides you talking to yourself in the RV?"

She shot him a look. "Yes, besides that. Any weird shadows?"

Romeo pursed his lips and glanced at the ceiling. "Nope." He became serious. "Did you?"

"I saw something that looked like a bird shadow floating behind me in the mirror." She shrugged. "But it wasn't actually there."

He put the last piece of bacon in his mouth and folded the whole thing over without breaking it. "Remember when our parents took us to Chuck E Cheese? I had nightmares about singing rats for weeks after that."

"But he's a mouse."

Romeo shrugged. "I'm only saying you're carrying all kinds of things in your head right now. There's a black bird on that business card you found, right? Maybe you're, uh...processing."

"I guess." Lily frowned and recalled the smoky taste like ash and something she couldn't place until that moment. Magic. *He wouldn't know anything about that, though.* "Still, I don't wanna hang around here longer than we have to, okay? Just in case."

"Sure. Let's get moving." They stood to clear their plates, and Romeo paused at the sink. "I know you're ready to do this for your mom, Lily. Would you be mad at me if I said I made us a little...itinerary on the way to Montreal?"

She blinked quickly and sipped her coffee. "As long as it's not Chuck E Cheese. Or too far out of the way."

"That's a no to both. I actually..." He scratched the back of his head. "I booked us an RV site at a campground when you were in the shower last night."

It felt like she was swallowing rocks instead of coffee. "A campground?"

"That's what we said we were doing," he reminded her and glanced over his shoulder at the front door. Julian was apparently still very much enjoying his breakfast out on the porch. "We might as well have some fun with it. And then, technically, it's not a lie."

"Romeo, that feels a little like playing around. And what if—" She glanced at the door too. "What if I get attacked again there? I don't know who's after me or if they're gonna follow us—"

"Are you any good at memory charms?"

"Well, yeah, but—"

"Hey, it's on the way. All right? It might add twenty minutes to drive off the highway when we get there tonight, but it's a lot better than spending the night in a Walmart parking lot."

She sighed. "True."

"And we'll be careful, okay? We'll keep our eyes open, look out for any...green fireballs. I got your back."

"Yeah, that's what worries me."

Romeo leaned toward her and smirked. "Trust me. It takes much more than a few spells to bring me down."

"What about the ones you haven't had to deal with yet?"

The front door opened, and Julian joined them in the kitchen to place his empty plate in the sink. "Y'all got everything you need?"

"Yeah, I think I covered it. It's cool that we don't need a tent or sleeping bags this time, right?" Romeo thunked a huge, heavy cooler onto the kitchen table and shrugged at Lily.

"What's that?"

"Food."

Her eyes widened. "Romeo, that's a ton of food. We're only gonna be on the road for, what? Two days?"

"Yep. And we need at least dinner tonight and break-fast tomorrow. Something tells me you don't keep the Winnie stocked up on a regular basis."

She stared at the cooler. "When did you put all that together?"

"This morning. I was up at six." When she gaped at him, he shrugged. "I know. I slept in." He hefted it off the table again, and the muscles bulged in his arm and shoulder despite the fact that he carried it like a stack of papers.

"I have to say I really appreciate your enthusiasm." Lily caught Julian smirking at her as she followed Romeo out the door. A dark shadow passed over the man's face, but when she looked again, it was gone. *Two shadows today? That can't be a coincidence.* "How are you feeling this morning, Julian?"

His eyebrows raised in surprise and she paused on her way out the door. "Fine. Right as rain. You know, Lily, I actually..." He chuckled. "I had a dream about your mama last night. Can you believe it? She showed up in my dream and told me thank you. That the two of y'all are doin' everything y'all need to do. Imagine that, right?" Lily looked blankly at him. "Oh, sure. I know dreams are only dreams. But it's comfortin' to imagine she's comin' to speak to me from the other side. You have any dreams like that?"

Nope. Because she's not dead. "I haven't yet. I bet it's nice, though."

"You don't let anything get in your way, Lily. Hear me? Dreams or no dreams."

"I never do."

"I know." He patted her shoulder. "I know." Romeo scrambled into the Winnebago with the cooler. His dad squinted at Lily against the morning sun, and he rubbed the back of his neck. "I ain't seen him this excited in a dog's age. You understand?"

She met his gaze and smiled. "How long, exactly, is a dog's age?"

Julian raised an eyebrow and pursed his lips, then smiled. "A long time. You always were a tonic for the boy in him, Lily. Might be you're bringing him the same thing now."

She returned his smile and glanced briefly at the blue morning sky. "Well, only if he can handle me."

He winked at her. "Attagirl."

"In all seriousness, though, I wouldn't be able to do any of this without him. Or you." She turned and wrapped her arms around his neck. The man smelled like bacon and coffee. "Thank you."

"Whatever for?" He sounded surprised, but he hugged her in return. It wasn't nearly as crushing as his regular embrace.

She pulled back and patted his shoulders. "For dinner. And breakfast."

"You mean supper?" She laughed. He raised his eyebrows and studied her gaze. "I ain't never seen a woman get all misty-eyed over a homecooked meal without it being about something else."

Lily tossed her head back and closed her stinging eyes to push away the tears that threatened. "Thanks for not giving up on me. Even after it seemed like I...well, when I stopped coming around."

Julian uttered a low hum. "Romeo told me this mornin' all about that damn misunderstandin' at County. I never blamed you one bit, but he doesn't anymore, either." She nodded. "Like I said, you're family. Don't be a stranger now, y'hear?"

"Yessir."

"There she is." He chucked her lightly under the chin and nodded at the Winnebago. "Aright, now git. Y'all have fun."

She headed toward the RV's open door and grasped both sides of the doorway firmly before she pulled herself up into the Winnie. Immediately, she caught sight of Romeo and rushed toward him. "Okay, hold on."

"What?" he said and spread his arms and chuckled from the driver's seat.

"I don't think you should be driving."

"Oh, come on. I've never driven one of these things before. I'm sure I can handle it."

She scrunched her nose and tilted her head as she studied him cautiously. "Yeah... But I kinda hope I'll be able to give her back to Bentley. You know, when things start looking up. So I want to keep her in good condition." He frowned at her, turned in the driver's seat, and gazed pointedly at the half-burned couch. "Okay, that's all superficial. It won't be if you drive it off a bridge."

"What makes you think I'd drive it off a bridge?" He laughed.

"Okay. I admit that maybe...I have a little...attachment to this thing, okay? She's gotten me through the lowest of lows in the last two months. I don't...feel ready to hand her over."

"Oh." He hadn't expected that but he conceded and

climbed out of the driver's seat. "Yeah, the Adventuremobile's all yours."

"Thank you. Hey, can you close the door, please?"

"Yep." Romeo stepped back through the RV and stuck his head out to call something to his dad.

Lily glanced back in the Winnie's side mirror and saw the man in the gray suit walking quickly down Ashley Avenue. He was small in the mirror but approached rapidly and it wouldn't take him long to cover the distance and be within range again. "Romeo. Close the door."

"Yeah, in a second. Dad, they've got a sale on shrimp—"

"I'm not messing around. Get in the RV and close the door."

The witch in the gray suit had almost reached the back of the Winnebago.

"Lily, it's fine. Only a—"

"Stay there!" She thrust the door open and jumped out of the driver's seat onto the street as she directed a powerful, crippling spell at the same witch who'd tried to kill her before. The maroon ball of magic careened into a car parked three houses down on the other side of the street. She gaped at the scene—no witch and no body, and only a dented minivan that blared its alarm for the whole neighborhood to hear.

"What was that?" Romeo ran around the front of the Winnebago and his eyes flashed silver to signal he was ready to turn if she needed him to. "What are you doing?"

"I..." Lily turned to look past him but didn't see

anyone. "Uh...the witch was back. That's why I told you to get back in the Winnie."

"And you took a shot at him?"

She scowled and tried to understand why the assassin would disappear—or if he had even been there at all. "No, I simply like to rack up insurance claims for fun." She gestured to the blaring minivan and the alarm cut off when she waved her hand at it. The dented metal eased itself back into the right shape, and the neighborhood fell silent. "So either I'm seeing things, or someone's trying to screw with me and kill me."

"That would be a lot of work." Romeo touched her shoulder. "We should go."

"Yeah. What about your dad?"

They moved cautiously around to the sidewalk. Julian leaned over the porch railing, shaking his head and laughing so hard, he didn't make a sound.

"Dad?"

"Go on," he wheezed. "Hoo, boy. Lily, sweetheart, you shoulda left that dent in the minivan."

She glanced at Romeo. "What?"

"Judy Rathbar might be the only person on this street who deserved that. The woman's been diggin' up my hydrangeas for years."

Frowning, Lily walked halfway up the path toward the porch so she didn't have to yell. "Did you see anybody walk down the street?"

"No."

"Okay." She turned to head back toward the Winnie's driver-side door. "Sorry about the...noise."

"Y'all have fun," Julian called from the porch.

"Hey, if you see anything...not right around here, will you give Romeo a call? Anything."

The man's eyes widened. "I'm fine, Lily."

"Please."

"Sure thing."

"Thanks. We'll see you soon."

She and Romeo climbed up into the Winnebago, and when they took their seats in the front, he stared at her for a minute. "Are you sure you're okay?"

"What? Yeah." Lily inserted the key and started the engine. "I'm ready to get outta here. I have a feeling there's kind of a time limit to the whole finding my mom thing."

"Didn't she used to time you on all those magic games you had to play?"

She gave him a nostalgic smile. "Yeah. She did."

"Then this won't be a problem at all."

EIGHT

Morning rush-hour traffic slowed them to a crawl before they'd even properly begun their journey. "I haven't left the city since I relocated to a house on wheels. I forgot how insane this traffic is." Lily peered through the wide windshield at the line of cars in front of them that all tried to get from Highway 17 to I-26.

"Nine-to-five commute." Romeo kicked his feet out in front of him—he only had enough space to mostly straighten them out—and put his hands behind his head. "I couldn't do that."

"So you don't."

"Don't what?"

She sighed. "Okay, please don't take this as an insult, but we never talked about it. Do you have a job?"

"Very direct." He grimaced. "I worked in construction."

After a hasty glance at him, she had to step on the gas

again and move into the small gap in front of them. She imagined him wearing a toolbelt and a hardhat, covered in sweat and cement dust, and had to shake the image out of her head before she started blushing.

"It was work."

"Not anymore?"

Romeo tilted his head and stared through the windshield. "The foreman couldn't handle losing to me at darts. And pool. Cornhole too, I think. A few times. After that, he really didn't like me and came up with some bullshit excuse to fire me."

"What?"

"Yeah."

"What did he say?"

"It doesn't matter."

"You know you can fight a wrongful termination, right?" She wanted to look at him for longer than two seconds, but the traffic had begun to move again.

"Yeah, but I'd rather not put this one in the spotlight."

"If it's a lie—"

"He said I was sleeping with his wife."

Lily frowned at the bumper in front of them. "That's so messed up. What kinda person does that?"

Romeo jerked forward and folded his arms. "I guess he was out of options or something. I don't know. And to be clear, I would never cross that line."

"Oh, I know."

"And his wife kinda looks like a man. She's missing a few teeth and everything too."

"Romeo, that's awful."

"You're tellin' me."

She laughed. "No, be nice. I can't believe someone would lie about something like that."

He shrugged. "I'm used to people making up all kinds of crap to get me off their hands."

Lily glanced at him from the corner of her eye but looked quickly back at the road. "I'm sorry."

"Don't be. It's all good now." His hands slapped down on the armrests. "I have a new job. On the open road."

Laughing, she readjusted her grip on the steering wheel. "I never said there was a paycheck in this."

"Not yet. But I know you'll get back on your feet when we find your mom. Gotta be some kinda reward, right?"

"When we find her, huh? I'm glad you share my optimism."

"I couldn't doubt you if I tried, Lily." He glanced at her with a broad smile.

"You're not seriously expecting a reward, though, right? I can't promise anything like that."

Romeo stared at her for a few seconds, then cleared his throat. "I'm trying to lighten things up a little. You look distracted."

"I am. I know the witch who attacked me in the garage was real because my spells hit him. So I'm having a hard time understanding why I'm seeing things all of a sudden."

"Well, I bet that when we get to this Magic Hat place in Montreal, you'll find some answers."

"It's called Le Chapeau Magique." Lily licked her lips and glanced at him.

"Only in French."

JUST PAST ST. George, Lily turned her blinker on to take the exit for I-95. Romeo jolted awake and sucked a sharp breath through his teeth when his shins smacked into the underside of the dash.

"What?" Lily shouted. "What's going on?"

"Where are we?"

"About to get on I-95."

"No." He grunted and pushed himself upright in the seat. "Turn your blinker off. We're not going that way."

"Why not? That's the fastest route."

"On a map, yeah." He ran a hand through his hair. "Not in traffic. That would take us through DC, Baltimore, Philly, and New York."

She continued to drive past the exit and frowned at him. "We're not camping upstate?"

"New York? No."

Lily squinted at the highway. "So...where are we going?"

Romeo leaned back in his seat and studied her. "Pennsylvania."

"Hmm. It sounds like that's far enough out of the way that we can avoid anybody stepping into friendly witch fire."

"That's exactly why I chose it. And it looks like a really cool site."

"And you planned all this while I was in the shower? I didn't think I took that long."

He inclined his head toward her. "It was the longest shower I've ever heard. But no. I got it all taken care of quickly."

"You know, I would have totally gone through all the big cities if you hadn't come with me. It's not very smart, now that I think about it."

"Lily, I told you, I got you. Travel agent. Navigator. Hey, I can add DJ to the list while we're at it."

She nodded. "Yeah. Music sounds good."

Romeo leaned forward to turn on the radio. The first thing to come through the speakers was merely static. He punched through the stations until music finally came on in the middle of a song. "Hey..." He grinned and nodded his head to the beat.

"What?" She glared at him. "You—no. I will zap you unconscious if you don't change the station right now."

"Not a fan of Nickelback, huh?"

"Are you?" He winked and they burst out laughing.

After flipping through a few more stations, he finally stopped on a song with far more banjo in it than she preferred. "There we go." He put his hands behind his head and leaned back in his seat again.

Lily shook her head and frowned through the windshield when the man's voice came through the Winnie's sound system—which was actually fairly decent. "Who is this?"

"You're kidding, right?" Romeo rolled his head sideways on the headrest to stare at her. "Mumford?"

"Uh...nope. Sorry."

"You've never heard Mumford and Sons? We're in the South, Lily."

"What, are they from here?"

Romeo chuckled. "Well, no. But they play all the time."

She merely widened her eyes and stared down the highway. The rising sun cast blinking shadows through the trees lining I-26. "I'm definitely getting the Southern feel. Feel free to leave it on this station." From the corner of her eye, she saw him lean back again with his hands behind his head, smiling. His eyes were closed, and the sunlight flashing across his tan skin and his nearly black hair almost made her forget to pay attention to the road. *Bluegrass. At least it's not country.*

SHE THOUGHT he'd fallen asleep again, but he told her to get off on I-77, and after three and a half hours of driving, they stopped at a gas station in Charlotte.

When she pulled up and turned the engine off, Romeo blinked, sat up straight, and looked around. "Why'd you stop?"

She stared at him. "It's a gas station."

"How'd this thing run out of gas in three hours?"

Lily unbuckled her seatbelt. "Probably because I haven't filled the tank on this thing since I got it. It's kinda nice when I literally don't have a drive home from downtown." She grabbed her purse and opened the door. "Do you want anything from inside?"

He almost fell out of his seat. "I got it. You fill up. What do you want?"

"Three Red Bulls."

"Three?"

"Yeah. We're not even a third of the way there, right? And I only had a half-full cup of coffee this morning." She smirked at him.

"Lily," he said with a laugh, "I can totally drive for a while if—"

"No, you were looking entirely too relaxed for me to make you drive the rest of the way." She grinned. "I still need a navigator and a DJ."

"Okay. Three Red Bulls coming up." His laughter echoed from inside the RV before she shut the door and focused on filling up the gas while he stepped inside.

She leaned against the side of the Winnebago and waited for the telltale click of a full tank. "All right. We don't have to watch those numbers next to the dollar sign, Lily. Try to ignore it." Folding her arms, she looked out over the trees and mountains in the distance. *Mom always said Charlotte was pretty.*

A plane moved slowly across the blue summer sky and she drew a deep breath of the humid air without the salt or the stink of pluff mud while she watched. "That's a big plane. Oh, crap. No, it's not—" The dark shape grew with incredible speed until she realized it was a bird. Against the late-morning sun, it looked completely black and its huge wings stretched wide.

The bird dove toward her. Lily ducked into a crouch and sent a minor deflection spell at the crazed avian. There was a metallic ping and a short-lived sizzle, then nothing. "Keep your eyes open, Lily," her mom used to say. "It's better to see the danger than to try hiding from it."

"I'm reasonably sure that didn't apply to dive-bombing attack birds," she muttered. But when she stood and looked around, there was no sign of the massive creature that had plunged out of the sky—no body, no feathers, nothing. She walked around the gas pump and even squatted to check under the Winnie. "I know I hit something." The something turned out to be the card reader on the gas pump, where she'd left a large black lump of dented metal. "Whoops." The gallon meter still ticked higher and higher, but the price numbers had stopped at a little over thirty-six dollars.

Lily tapped it a few times, but the numbers didn't move with the gallons of gas that pumped into the tank. She squinted at the meter again. "Well, guess I won't know how much it is until I get that receipt." The gas nozzle clicked, the pump stopped, and she returned it to the cradle. "It is so weird that I'm turning into a person who prints receipts now. But hey, when money's tight, you do what you gotta do." She punched the print receipt button and took the printed slip.

"All full?" Romeo leaned against the back corner of the Winnie with a huge brown paper bag tucked under one arm.

"Yep."

"Great." He disappeared behind the back of the RV and she heard the door open and shut behind him.

When she glanced at the receipt in her hand, she had to look long and hard to overcome her disbelief. Thirty-six dollars to fill up an eighty-gallon tank. "Well, I appreciate the generosity. I'll have to come back here when it's safe and pay them back." She stuck the receipt in her purse, climbed into the driver's seat, and puffed a sigh. Romeo didn't even have to ask what was going on. "I think I had another hallucination."

His mouth dropped open and he looked cautiously at her. "What?"

She returned his look with an airy gesture. "A big black something with wings fell out of the sky and went all Angry Birds on me."

"I...can't tell if you're serious or not right now."

She took a deep breath and buckled her seatbelt. "I can't tell if someone's trying to hurt me or send me a message, or if I cracked and all my sanity's spilling out like egg yolk."

"That's quite the image. But it's definitely not number three."

"I know. But I... Mom never quite ran me through how to unscramble incredibly real visions into something I can actually work with. That bird wasn't real, Romeo. I would've hit it with my spell, but it vanished completely, exactly like the witch in front of your house. Did you know your dad had a dream about her last night?"

"Who?"

"My mom."

He shrugged. "It doesn't surprise me."

"Yeah, but he thinks she's dead like everyone else does."

"I'd probably dream about you all the time if I thought you were dead."

"Wow. That's a morosely flattering thing to say."

"You're welcome."

Lily started the engine and accelerated toward the highway. "I don't know. I keep thinking she's trying to tell me something, wherever she is, and somebody else keeps getting in the way. You know, mixing up all her messages."

"Like a magical radio jammer?"

"Sure."

Chuckling, he ripped open the Slim Jims he'd bought from the gas station and offered her one.

She did a double-take and laughed. "Okay, we're on a road trip, but we're definitely not twelve."

"Oh, come on. You love these."

"I used to." She eyed the brown bag between his feet. "Did you get my Red Bulls."

"All three. Pace yourself."

"I'll have you know I can hold my caffeine and taurine very well." The can hissed as he cracked it open for her. She took it from him and drank as much as she could before she had to look at the road and set the can in the cupholder. "You know, this would go really well with one of your meat sticks."

"My what, now?"

She snorted. "Slim Jim. Please." The minute she held out her hand again, she felt the thin packaging in her palm and brought it up to yank at the casing with her teeth. "We had it really good when we were twelve, didn't we?"

"The best. It doesn't quite hold up to now, though." Romeo cast her a sidelong glance and her cheeks hurt with how much she was smiling.

NINE

Three hours later, Lily pulled off I-81 outside Roanoke, Virginia. Barely five minutes after cracking open the second energy drink, she thought her bladder was about to burst.

"I thought—" Romeo shook his head and snorted. "I thought you could handle your caffeine." His long strides easily matched her speed-walking into the gas station.

"Six hours on the road and this is my first bathroom break." She looked at him, nodded curtly, and tried not to dance when he opened the door for her. "And I waited until we stopped for lunch."

When she was finished—vastly relieved but still a little jittery and definitely hungry—she searched for her companion in the gas station, but he wasn't there. Instead, he leaned against the Winnie with his arms folded. "Okay," she said as she reached him. "Are we stopping for lunch? Or do we go through that monster cooler you packed so quickly this morning?"

He nodded toward the other end of the parking lot. "When was the last time you ate at a Burger King."

"Uh...probably with you."

"Look at this." Romeo walked backward and threw his arms out. "On the open road. We're not running away from anything but toward your mom, right? And it's a walk down memory lane."

She shook her head but moved quickly to keep up with him. "You're awfully excited about this."

"I'm only trying to lighten the mood, Lily. That's what friends are for. And Whoppers. Plus, I'm trying to stay one step ahead of the game here. You wouldn't like me when I'm hangry." He winked and turned in time to open the door for her.

"Okay, but at least let me buy lunch."

"Nope."

"You bought all my energy drinks. And I ate your snacks."

He put a hand on her back and guided her toward the counter. She tried not to look at his arm halfway around her. "I know all that wasn't even close to how much you spent on gas."

"Actually..." The receipt was right on top of all the junk in her purse. He followed the direction of her gaze and peered inside.

"Did you do that on purpose?" he asked, surprise in his tone.

"Of course I—" She ducked and lowered her voice. "Of course I didn't do it on purpose. That's what I was saying. I aimed for the bird, but it wasn't a bird. Because I ended up...well...putting a hold on all gas charges." He snorted, glanced at the other customers, and nodded at her purse. She closed it quickly. "I'm gonna pay them back. When I can."

"Okay, then. In that case, if you still insist on buying me lunch, your wish is my command." His comically over-done bow made her roll her eyes.

"All right. You know, the last time I remember eating at one of these with you, your father put away four of those giant burgers."

"Yeah, only because he was pissed that his own son could pack away more food than he could."

"Okay," Romeo said through a mouthful of his second Whopper. "I have a whole new appreciation for my dad in this moment. I bought a third burger. There is no way I can eat it."

"You killed an entire large fries, though." Lily gestured to the array of wrappers and fried crumbs between them.

A huge belch escaped him, which he cut off halfway through with a fist to his mouth and an expression of morti-fication. "I am so sorry." A flush crept up his neck.

"Hey, if I ate what you did, I'd be lettin' 'em out too."

He stared at her, his eyes a little hazy. "You're amazing."

"Ha. Thanks."

"How was your meal?"

She shrugged. "Road-trip quality."

"Excellent."

They cleaned up and headed to the Winnebago, making it a twenty-five-minute pit stop before they set off again. For the next four hours, they drove north on I-81 in virtually a straight line through Virginia and a tiny part of Maryland until they reached Pennsylvania. Romeo pulled out his phone when they couldn't find a good radio station, and once he hooked it up to the Winnie's dash, he played the weirdest collection of music in existence—Guns N' Roses, Norah Jones, Johnny Cash, Queen, Imagine Dragons, and Pink Floyd—and those were only the names she knew. "Okay, did you make a playlist deliberately to mess with me?"

When he looked up from his phone, his gaze was blank like she'd yanked him out of a deep reverie. "No. It's on shuffle." She laughed. "All right. What are you into, then?"

She drummed her fingers on the steering wheel. "Got any Grateful Dead?"

"Really?" He leaned forward to stare at her.

"Yeah, really. You know who they are, right?"

"Please. You do know there's a Dead tribute band that plays at Pour House all the time?"

"Oh, yeah. I've been often. There's nothing like the real deal, though."

"It's literally impossible that you saw them live."

She shook her head and chuckled. "I didn't." "Friend of the Devil" played through the speakers now, and he leaned back again. "I've been to any number of shows, though."

"Okay. What's the best one you've ever seen?"

"The best?" She took a deep breath. "Well, if we're going with all around most fun..."

"Yeah, go with that."

"I saw Phish at Madison Square Gardens. My mom got us a suite at The New Yorker for...I dunno. Three or four nights—"

"Of course she did." He shook his head but a trace of a smile played around his mouth.

"What, is that bad?"

He laughed. "Absolutely not. Are you kidding me? You know, I think this is the first time in my life that I'm actually jealous of you."

Lily refocused on the highway. "Don't say that. It's the weirdest way to compliment somebody."

"Well, you're welcome."

"Hey, is that the exit?"

His gaze lingered on her for a few more seconds. Her cheeks grew a little hot but he turned away from her slowly to lean back in his seat. "Thirty-seven. Yep."

She took the exit onto Highway 233, and after about five minutes, they drove between green trees that towered above them on either side. Romeo rolled his window down, stuck his face out into the air, and took a long sniff.

"Hey, roll up the window," she said.

"Why?"

"It's...muggy."

He flashed her a befuddled look. "We're camping, Lily."

"We're passing through."

"You can't roll up the window on the air when you're camping."

She wanted to look at him but the road was now a little bumpy. Then, she laughed. "I've lived on generator-powered AC in a motorhome for two months too long."

"Yep. Don't worry. I won't hold it against you."

"Oh, well thank you very much. Okay, where are we supposed to go now?"

"Look at this," Romeo exclaimed when she pulled up to their reserved RV site. "Electrical hookups and everything. And right next to the water pump."

"Great. We'll be everyone's most popular neighbors."

He peered through the windshield and his window. "It won't be that bad. I've only seen two other RVs here. Hey, they might be some of your people."

"My people?"

"Yeah. Your boondocker tribe." His face was so serious, Lily thought she'd missed something.

"Oh, I get it. You're messing with me."

"We could do a little boondocking on this trip, you know." He grinned.

"I don't know."

"Yeah. Sneaking into places we're not supposed to be in. Parking out in the middle of nowhere—"

"Romeo, that's not what I've been doing for two months."

"But wouldn't it be fun?"

"Okay, I tell you what. Once we find my mom and everything's back to normal, you can park this thing wherever you want."

He barked out a laugh.

Lily stared at him. "I mean—wait. You know what I mean."

"I sure do. And wherever we go, I promise, I'll make sure to keep the raccoons away."

Her mouth dropped open but she managed no reply. Finally, she bit her lip and laughed with him. "I was nine."

"It's still hilarious." He unbuckled his seatbelt and stood. "Come show me how to hook this thing up."

The campsite really was beautiful. Once they had hooked up the Winnie, Lily stood in silence to take it all in. The vista was uncluttered, grass and dirt paths and forest, which were easier to appreciate without a campsite full of RVs. Romeo stepped out of the vehicle with the giant cooler.

"Where are you taking that?"

"Picnic table," he shouted without a backward glance.

"He's turning this into a real camping trip." She laughed in surprise and slapped at the mosquito that landed on her arm. "Did you bring any bug spray?"

"Oh. Uh...no. I don't really ever use it." He opened the cooler.

"Why not?"

"Mosquitos tend to stay away from me, I guess," he said with a shrug. "Ticks, on the other hand... Well, I've gotten good at checking for ticks."

"Big problem, huh?"

"Yeah." He stopped pulling things out of the cooler to scratch behind his ear. "They're a lot easier to catch when I'm...you know. Running around on four legs."

"Have you ever tried a tick collar?"

"What?"

"I'm kidding. I know that's totally out of the question."

He looked at her briefly and smirked. "Yeah, I don't do collars."

Lily selected one of the bottled waters he'd bought from the last gas station and set out for dinner.

He paused and shrugged. "Not unless it comes with a ball gag."

She choked on her water, forced herself to swallow, and coughed a few times.

"Hey, look at us. We're both kidding." He shrugged with a goofy grin and it turned to worry when she didn't stop coughing. "Woah, sorry. Are you okay?"

"Yeah. I just..." She gestured toward her throat and took another sip. "I'm fine. You got me on that one."

After he'd studied her for a few more seconds, he clapped, rubbed his hands together, and grinned at the spread he'd laid out beside the cooler. "Dinner."

Lily stepped over the bench to sit and examined everything he'd put out—potato salad, macaroni salad, two wrapped summer sausages, a wheel of brie cheese, Wheat Thins, and cold baked beans. "Um..."

"What's up?"

"I hate to sound ungrateful, because I'm not. But I think you forgot something."

"Such as?"

"Vegetables. Maybe."

Romeo's nose twitched in his obvious attempt not to look disgusted. "I'm not really big on the rabbit food. Unless it's collards."

She bit her lip and winced a little but tried to make light of it. "You know, that's one thing I kinda hoped you'd grown out of."

"My dad never grew out of it. I guess it's in the wolf blood." He shrugged and peeled off the casing of one of the summer sausages. "Which is totally weird, but I can't really do anything about it."

"Hey, I'm not trying to change you. I can do with whatever whenever." She picked up the baked beans and jerked the lid off. A spray of condensation and a sludge of cold sauce spewed across the table. She jumped when a few drops splattered across her cheek and her mouth made an 'O' of surprise.

He looked up from the massive pile of potato salad he'd heaped onto his own plate, studied her for a moment, and broke into wild laughter. He leaned so far back on the bench, she expected him to fall into the dirt.

"I think you might've packed this one a little too full." She giggled and wiped the splintering wooden table with a paper towel. "It's been a long time since I've driven through rising elevation—"

Romeo stood quickly from the table and leaned almost all the way over it toward her to wipe the spray of bean sauce off her cheek. He plopped back onto the bench, sucked the sauce off his finger, and tipped his head in consideration. "That's good stuff. And you're wasting it on a paper towel."

"What?" She spread her arms wide and grinned. "There's so much more still left in the container."

"Yeah, and it's all gonna get eaten when we're done. I might not have brought any vegetables, but come on. Baked beans are life."

"Out of all the possible choices, you're in love with baked beans."

"Well, yeah."

"Okay. Have some more." With a giggle, she flicked her finger in the direction of the baked beans. Another spray of it launched from the container and splattered across his white t-shirt, up his neck, and a little into the hair that curled below his ears. A shriek of surprised laughter escaped her, and he spread his arms as he looked at the mess. "I'm sorry," she said through another fit of giggles. "I didn't...I was trying to be funny."

"Well, that worked." He looked challengingly at her and his Adam's apple bobbed up and down with silent laughter. "Good thing I love beans."

"That's what I was thinking. Oh...here." Lily grabbed another paper towel as she stood and swung her legs over the bench. She poured water on it and walked around the table toward him. "Yes, I covered you in sauce. But I'm not too proud to clean up my messes." Romeo turned to face her, swung one leg over the back of the bench, and scooped a huge chunk of beans off his chest to flick it into the dirt. Lily exploded into laughter again.

"Seriously, I was not trying to make it this bad." She

put one hand on his shoulder to steady herself as she leaned down to wipe as much sauce as she could off his shirt. "You did bring more than one shirt, right?" The paper towel in her hand moved up to wipe the sludge from his neck.

"Do you think I only own one shirt?" His voice was so low, she could've sworn she felt it vibrate through his shoulder and into her hand.

When she looked at him, her gaze flickered away again, out of her control, but she forced it back. "No..." They were so close, she could see the specks of gold in his green eyes. She paused in wiping his neck and only then did she realize that she stood with one foot on either side of his leg, practically straddling him.

Romeo moved his hand to where she still pressed the wet paper towel against his neck and stared at her the whole time. His fingers settled on hers for the longest second before he slipped the paper towel out of her hand and tossed it onto the table. "I brought at least three." It came out somewhere between a whisper and a growl.

Lily blinked. "What?"

"Shirts." He leaned away from her and grasped the hem of his t-shirt with both hands.

She stepped back in time to avoid being clipped by his elbows when he lifted the garment over his head in one fluid motion. "You didn't have to...change right here—" She took a deep breath and stared at his six-pack and his chest and his shoulders that were all as tanned as the rest of him. He stood, and she realized she was staring. Her gut reaction was to lean over the bench, grab a piece of the summer sausage he'd already cut, and shove it into her mouth.

Romeo's other leg swung over the bench, and he leaned toward her to say, "I'll go into the Winnie, then."

"Yep," she responded through chewing, unable to look at him. When she heard the Winnebago's door open and shut again, she released a huge sigh and swallowed the mouthful. "Okay, I know kids grow up, but come on. Is it supposed to be this hot in the woods after dinner?"

TEN

"We should take a hike," Romeo said after dinner as he shut the fridge and turned toward her. Lily closed the door to the trash cabinet and stared at him. "Seriously. It'll be fun."

"Yeah, my legs could use a stretch. But...we have to be careful, okay?"

"I'm an expert at being careful." His shoe caught on the edge of the cabinets, and he stumbled toward her with a grunt. "Okay. Except for that."

"You know what I mean." She glanced through the RV's windows at the empty campground. "If we see any people, it's probably best to stay away from them for now. And if anything weird happens—"

"I know. You don't want anyone to be hurt." He stepped really close and put his hands on her shoulders. "Neither do I. But we're halfway there, and nothing's happened so far. Can you try to relax a little and forget about what might happen?"

She puffed a slightly irritated breath. "I can try to relax. Not so good at the 'not thinking about the future' part." *I have Mom to thank for that. I wish I could let it go sometimes.*

"Awesome. That's all we need." Romeo released her and stepped back. "Let's go to the lake."

"I think it was more of a stale pond that we passed on the way here."

"No, not that one. There's an actual lake ten minutes up the trail."

"Wow, you really did all kinds of research for this one."

"Well..." Romeo opened the fridge and reached inside. "I wanted to make sure it was something special. You know, all those summers you missed with me and Dad. Wanna know the best part?"

"That's a silly question."

He removed his hand, closed the fridge, and lifted a six-pack of PBR. His grin broad, he swung it triumphantly. "I told you the first thing we were gonna do was stop and buy some."

"When did you get those?" She couldn't decide whether to laugh or try to shove them back into the fridge.

"At the first stop. When you had that weird...non-bird attack."

"Yeah, I was a little distracted."

"And now it's time to focus. On relaxing."

She shot him a look and he shook his head.

"You get the picture. Let's go." Nodding toward the door, Romeo gripped the plastic six-pack rings with one hand and moved toward her.

Lily leaned away and fixed him with an enquiring look. "Wait. Did you maybe get something else a little more—"

"This is what we got, my friend. You're gonna love it. Come on, come on."

She laughed. "Hold on a sec. Let me—oh!" Turning away from him at the last second saved her from being chest-bumped at the top of the two stairs. "Okay, okay." Giggling, she moved quickly down to open the door and hop outside. Romeo's long legs made his fluid step down onto the dirt look like he somehow hovered out of the RV, and she shut the door behind him.

"We're moving," he called and shook his head. "Keep up. Come on. We're not stoppin' now."

Lily hurried to catch up with him. "I don't know if being an unstoppable force is the right way to focus on relaxing."

He tipped his head to regard her with an amused expression. "I'm only trying to get to the calm tranquility a little faster."

"Yeah, and you're really fast. But—" She laughed and brushed the hair away from her eyes. "Maybe take it down a notch so I can keep up with all your tranquility." He grinned at her but slowed enough that she could match his pace. "Thank you. So, hey. When was the last time you went camping?"

Romeo looked ahead down the path through the trees as he pulled one beer away from the others. "I dunno. Sophomore year, probably. My dad stopped wanting to put all the effort into anything beyond staying in his cousin's cabin, you know? Then, he eventually lost the energy for that too. Did you and your mom ever go to any fancy camp-sites? Stay in a lodge or something?"

Lily frowned at the dirt path in front of them. "I can't say we ever stayed in a fancy lodge. I think that's mostly a hunter thing."

"Sure."

"Actually, I think it was the last time we all went together. You, me, and our parents. That was right before high school, wasn't it?"

"Yep. I think so." There was a short crack, hiss, and pop of a can opening. Romeo thrust the can in front of her before she had the chance to look at him.

"Uh...I'm gonna have to work up a thirst for that stuff first."

"Aw. I know you're only trying to be nice." He raised the can in a silent toast and took a few long chugs. It was incredibly loud amid the buzzing of all the insects in the trees and the few crickets singing as the sun headed down. He exhaled a massive sigh and smacked his lips.

"That doesn't make you sick? To hike and throw back a brew?"

"I assume you haven't been on a hike since you reached the legal drinking age." His head wobbled a little in a mockery of that law.

"Neither have you."

"I said I haven't been camping since sophomore year. I hike all the time."

"Huh."

"Okay...nature walks. Whatever. The point is"—he

held the beer can out in front of him like he was making a toast—"there is nothing like drinking a cold one on a hike."

"That, to me, sounds worse than doing a kegstand."

"Only until you get good at it." He turned the beer up one more time, drank the remainder in a few swallows, and nodded. "I'll let you give it a shot on the way back."

"You know, your generosity astounds me."

"I try."

When the wooded path ended and they finally came out beside the lake, Lily was surprised to see so many people there. "Okay, this is the weirdest combination of people I have ever seen. What is going on?"

Romeo paused beside her, crushed the beer can, and tossed it into the trash receptacle next to the closest picnic table. "I have no idea. It smells like a group of witches, though."

"You know, even if I didn't already know werewolves can smell magic, I'd still have to agree with you. But I'm really confused."

The lake was big although the prime location was right there on the beach for about half a mile on either side of the path. On their right, a group of a dozen witches were gathered. Most of them sat in beach chairs or on towels but a few of them splashed in the lake and shrieked. They were around Lily and Romeo's age, drinking and blaring obnoxiously loud party music over the water.

To Lily's left and quite a way farther from the path than the partiers, a smaller coven of seven sat in a circle on the beach. They'd built a fire in the center of their circle and all of them were dressed in various shades of white and cream. Two women had flower crowns in their hair. They laughed, talked quietly, broke out into occasional rounds of light laughter, and completely ignored the opposite energy that bounced around the partiers a mile down the lakeshore.

"I think that spot would be perfect," Romeo said and pointed directly ahead at the lone wooden bench on the beach.

She squinted against the sun's glare reflected on the water. "Right in the middle, huh?"

He looked at her and leaned against her shoulder. "Hey, relaxing, remember?"

"This is a lot of people—"

"And all of them are witches. Probably not as scary as you, though." She glanced at him and he nodded, eager to convince her he meant it. "But if anything followed us here, which I doubt, at least you have backup."

Lily glanced at both witch covens and frowned. "That's a good point. So the music's not gonna bother you if you're trying to relax?"

"No."

"What about the screaming?"

"Not really."

She looked out along the shore to their left, past the circle of the white-wearing coven. "There's another bench over there. That's what? Another ten-minute walk? I don't mind going a little farther if it's quieter. And maybe a little more...I dunno. Not so centrally located."

"But this spot's gonna have the best view of the sunset."

"Oh." She gazed across the lake. "You want to watch the sunset." He grinned, nodded toward the bench, and headed toward it. "Okay. Then I guess the middle is exactly where we need to be."

She sat beside him, still with two feet of splintered, sun-bleached wood between them. Romeo leaned over the side of the bench to set the rest of the beers in the sand and worked on the one in his hand. Lily stared across the lake.

The summer bugs hummed around them. The sky took on a golden hue in the west when the sun hit the tips of the trees. Music pumped from the speakers on their right, punctuated by explosive laughter, screams of delight, splashing, and sounds of men's voices rising in rowdy excitement. Someone on that side uttered a wild whoop, followed by a huge splash, and the rest of the little get-together cheered.

A soft chant in low tones rose from their left. Lily glanced over her shoulder to see the coven of witches dressed in white and cream all resting the backs of their hands on their knees, their eyes closed, to begin their own ritual. A bright green flash of light leapt from one witch's open palm into the hand of the person beside her. "How do they focus with all this noise?"

"Because they're so relaxed," Romeo said right in her ear.

She jumped and leaned away from him. "Okay. I think I'm starting to get the message." They smiled at each other but she had to look away. *I don't wanna get too relaxed.* She took a deep breath. "So I wondered—"

"I thought of something—" He'd turned to face her too,

and they both stopped, laughed, and lowered their gazes. "Sorry." Romeo dipped his head toward her. "You go first."

"No, go ahead."

His green eyes glowed in the sunset's golden light—not the way they changed before he was about to shift but almost the same. He chuckled softly, his mouth twisting in a self-conscious half smile, and stared at the space of bench between them. "I was trying to think of a few ways to...I dunno. Make this a little easier for you."

Lily bit her lip. "That's really sweet and I appreciate it. But I'm totally fine."

"No, I meant make it easier for you here." Romeo patted his chest over his heart and leaned down toward her face. "I mean, if you want to talk about walking in your shoes. No, it's not the same thing, but I get what it's like to know the truth when nobody else in the world believes you. It's a...tough road."

Nodding, she felt herself sucked into his gaze. "When they took you in for something you didn't do."

He swallowed. "Yep. I don't pray or anything, but I thought witches had something almost like it. Am I making sense?"

"I—" Lily smiled. "Yeah. You mean like a guidance ritual?"

His eyes widened with his smile. "Do you know one?"

"I know a few."

"Okay." Romeo slapped his hands down on his knees, studied her for a few seconds, and stood. "Okay. Can you give me, like...a couple minutes?"

Curious, she tilted her head and shrugged. "Sure."

"I'll be right back. Just...I'll be back." He nodded, tossed back the rest of his beer, and hurried toward the coven seated around the fire.

"Wait. Romeo, I don't know if that's such a good idea." She turned on the bench to watch him stroll across the sand toward the witch coven in white. He turned back once to nod and raised a finger for her to wait. She leaned over the bench. "Romeo." It wasn't exactly a shout, but it was loud enough to lift her voice above the pounding music on her right. "I can't start shouting in the middle of their ceremony," she muttered. "What's he doing?"

He'd reached the circle now and spoke softly to the witches seated in the sand. They all looked at him, cautious of the werewolf who had approached them and a little concerned as to why. When he gestured toward Lily, they looked at her. She grinned and grasped the back of the bench with one hand while she raised the other in a tentative wave. "I promise he's not gonna cause any trouble..." she muttered through her grin. A few witches nodded at her and smiles bloomed on their faces. One woman wearing a flower crown said something to Romeo and waved a hand at the sand beside her. He looked at Lily one last time, gave her an excited wave, and hunkered into a squat at the edge of the coven's circle.

"Please give him a chance all the way through," she whispered.

"Dick move, right?"

Frowning, she turned slowly to see one of the raucous partiers standing in front of the empty seat on the bench. The guy was dripping wet in regular shorts—not swimming trunks—and his soaked hair stood on end in hundreds of spikes when he ran a hand through it. "I'm sorry?"

He nodded toward Romeo and the other coven. "Leaving you here for that bunch of light-lovers."

"I'm gonna go ahead and choose to believe you're not insulting that coven. And he didn't leave me." She smiled and raised her eyebrows. "Thanks for the concern, but I'm fine."

"Well, if I was sitting here next to you, I wouldn't get up again unless I was taking you with me." With that, he actually sat—a lot closer than Romeo had—and dropped his arm onto the back of the bench behind her.

Lily stood and turned to face him. "That's not gonna happen," she said. "I'm asking you nicely to please go back to your party."

"Relax, babe."

"Excuse me?"

"Kevin!"

Both Lily and this way too cocky jerk turned toward the rowdy group drinking and dancing on the beach. "Yeah, gimme a second," he shouted in response.

Lily stared at the other witches. One of them was putting on a lightshow and multi-colored sparks erupted from his hands in twisting patterns.

"I didn't get your name," Kevin said, still lounging on the bench.

"That's because I didn't give it to you."

The guy's self-absorbed smirk faded.

"Seriously, Kevin! What the hell?"

"You should go back." She gestured toward the

partying witches. He studied her with arrogant appreciation and licked his lips. "And if you look at me like that again, I won't be this nice."

"I'm only tryin' to show you a good time, babe. You look like you could use it."

"You look like I'm about to teach you a really important lesson, Kevin."

"She doesn't need anything from you." Romeo stopped on the other side of her and scowled at the intruder.

"Are you sure about that?" Kevin stood with a ridiculous swagger and swiveled his head as he stepped forward. " 'Cause from where I'm standing, it looks like she's starting to regret picking your stray-mutt ass off the side of the road."

"No, it doesn't," Lily said, but both of them ignored her.

Romeo growled and his upper lip twitched into a sneer. He had at least three inches on the idiot, but the other guy obviously didn't care. "Oh, yeah," Kevin said, his eyebrows raised. "I know exactly what you are, wolf. And now I wonder why the hell you thought you'd be welcome here."

The were's chest swelled with a long, deep breath and his nostrils flared.

"Because you're not," the other man added.

Lily glanced from one to the other and scowled. "Okay, we need to call this off right now. Romeo—"

"She's not going anywhere with you." Romeo's green eyes flashed into rings of silver.

"I think she will," the guy said, "once I'm done with you."

"She can make her own decisions, thanks." She stepped toward them and glared at the two testosterone-pumped idiots. Neither of them looked at her until she placed a hand on each of their shoulders and gave them both a gentle nudge backward. Not enough to push them away, but it got their attention. "Nobody's fighting over me. So let's walk away and get on with our night, huh?"

Kevin sucked his teeth and raised his eyebrows at Romeo again. "Sounds good to me." He caught her completely by surprise when he turned, wrapped his arm around her shoulders, and pulled her forward with him.

The force of it was so strong that she stumbled out of her flats and her bare feet sank into the sand. "What are you—" She heard Romeo growl behind them before eleven years of training kicked in. Lily stepped in front of this douchebag with his arm around her and grabbed the hand dangling over her shoulder with both her own. In one fluid movement, she bent and jerked down hard. Kevin catapulted over her shoulder to land on the beach with a grunt and a dull thud.

A round of surprised jeers rose from his friends, but none of them cared enough to help him. He stared stupidly at the sky with a little gasp, and she stepped toward his head. When she leaned over him, his eyes widened with alarm. "That is so not what I meant," she said and summoned a ball of crackling green energy in her hand. "I have no intention of going anywhere with you so quit being a moron. I don't want to have to hurt you even worse." Without waiting for a reply, she spun and walked quickly across the sand, stopping only to snatch her flats off the beach.

"Dude," one of the partying witches shouted. "You got your ass handed to you by a—"

"Shut up." Kevin didn't mean for everyone to hear his bruised ego, but the lake made it echo everywhere.

Lily stormed past Romeo, who'd stopped in his tracks after she'd handled Kevin on her own. From the corner of her eye, she saw him gaping at her with a slack jaw. "Screw it." Dropping into a squat, she ripped a can of PBR from the plastic rings, stood as she cracked it open, and chugged as much of it as she could in one breath. She grimaced at the taste but it didn't stop her from taking her seat again on the bench and swallowing another huge gulp.

ELEVEN

A few seconds later, Romeo approached her slowly and hesitated at the bench. Both groups of witches had already gone back to their own festivities as if Lily's little smack-down never happened. "Can I sit?"

She looked up and immediately noticed his concerned frown. "I think I made my point. So yes. Yes, you can. And for the record, you don't ever have to ask me that."

He sighed. "That's good to know." He sat much closer than before and ran a hand through his curls. "So, I have to admit...when I imagined getting you to drink a PBR with me, it went a little differently in my head."

Lily uttered a wry chuckle and lifted the beer can to look at it. "It's not that bad. Honestly, it tastes better as a pat on the back." He snorted and she stared out across the lake that now reflected bright orange and the first traces of pink in the sky.

"I was only trying to help." He leaned forward to prop his forearms on his thighs. "To stand up for you, I guess."

"I know. I appreciate it. Really. But I can stand up for myself."

"Clearly. Is that the first time you've ever actually used those moves outside the dojo?"

"Mom didn't have a dojo."

"You know what I mean."

She glanced at the sky and smirked. "Maybe. But it was worth it." Now that her irritation had drained away, she turned to look at him. "Romeo, I didn't ask you to come with me because I need protection or someone to fight my battles."

"I know."

"Good. Because I missed you." His green eyes searched hers intently. "And I'm really glad I didn't have to ask you to come with me. I don't think I could have."

"I know."

Lily laughed and glanced at the orange-and-red-stained lake. "It's so weird to think about now. No matter what I did to be better, or how many people I tried to help, I still spent the last seven years surrounded by all these important, rich, fancy people, and none of them actually cared about me. Honestly, the only time I didn't feel alone was when my mom came home from her trips. Until we find her...you're the only person who knows who I really am." She met his gaze. "You always were."

Romeo took a deep breath and released it slowly. "I know."

"You maybe wanna switch up the dialogue a little bit, or—"

"Hey, you're taking the words right outta my mouth. And it's not with magic."

Her heart fluttered in her chest and she couldn't help but smile. "Maybe a little magic."

"I don't think so."

"Yeah, just not the spell kind."

"Lily, you've always been my best friend," he added with a little frown. "Even when we weren't talking. You know that, right?"

She grinned at him. "I know."

"Oh, yeah." Romeo straightened quickly and reached over the side of the bench.

"I'm good, thanks. I still have half a beer left."

"You—oh. No." He laughed. "It's not a beer." He turned a little on the bench and offered her a tall white pillared candle.

Lily had no idea what it was for, and her confusion brought her smile back. "Oh...is this what the nice witch coven gave you?"

"Yup." He nodded at the circle of witches in flowing white clothes and flower crowns around the fire.

She glanced at them—they all had their eyes closed again and muttered in low tones—and looked cautiously at him. "They didn't give you any trouble, did they? A werewolf in a witch coven and everything?"

"Hey, I can take care of myself too, you know. And no. No trouble. They didn't even care, honestly."

"That is awesome."

"So that guidance ritual you mentioned." Romeo glanced at the lake and the forest around them. Everything had cooled noticeably now with the fading light. "I assume that's why they handed me a candle. This is one of the best nights to do it on, don't you think?"

Lily raised her eyebrows. "Really?"

He thought she was joking at first, but then he stopped laughing. "It's the twenty-first. Of June..." She gave him a clueless shrug. "Lily, the Summer Solstice."

"Oh, my God." A laugh escaped her, and she doubled over in surprise and embarrassment. "I totally...I didn't even think about it."

"So, admittedly, it might not be as important as not getting killed by rogue witches in business suits who also show up as visions. It's understandable that you forgot. I guess that's why you have me now to remind you." He chuckled and nodded toward the lake. "Are you up for this?"

"Absolutely. It is kinda perfect."

They moved toward the water together and stopped at the edge of the lake, digging their toes into the damp sand. Romeo turned toward her and held the candle between them in both hands. "Like I said, I don't pray." He licked his lips and sighed. "So I'll simply follow your lead. Oh, I almost forgot. The witches put this on here for you." He turned the candle so Lily could see the rune etched into the white wax. "I guess it's supposed to mean—"

"Freedom."

When he looked at her, his eyes were wide above a soft, compassionate smile. "I'm not telling you what to do or anything. I only thought maybe it—"

"It's perfect." She raised a hand to snap over the candle

and the unburned wick burst into flame. "My mom and I did this once after my grandma passed. Mom didn't quite know how to handle things for a while, so she asked for all kinds of guidance. I'm reasonably sure I remember how it's done. Intention over results, right?" She smiled at him and shrugged.

"You're running the show here." He nodded.

"Right. Can you hold it there for me?" Lily took a deep breath and drew a circle in the air around the bottom of the candle. She pressed her palm up against the base and looked at him.

"You're gonna have to walk me through whatever comes next," he said with a chuckle.

"Okay. So now we send it off into the lake." She wrapped her hands around the candle and her fingers brushed against his before he released it carefully. A few steps brought her to the water's edge and she knelt in the sand and grimaced when the damp soaked through her thin joggers. He knelt beside her and she leaned forward to place the candle on the water's surface. She removed her hands slowly and laughed again when the candle floated effortlessly without sinking or wobbling. "I call on the spirits of the North, the South, the East, the West. On Mother Moon and Father Sun. On the god-goddess and earth and time. Guide me through my journey. Show me what I need to see." Romeo echoed every word softly, and she grinned.

She raised a finger and tapped the white candle gently. A golden glow spread like ripples at the contact and the candle floated away from them toward the middle of the lake. The daylight had all but completely faded now and threw dim hues of faded pink and dark purple into the sky. The ritual candle drifted across the water and the single flame flickered brighter than it should have—one simple request. Sometimes, it gave one simple answer.

When she looked at Romeo again, he stared at the candle on the darkening waters. She shifted on the sand and scooted closer to him until the edge of her thigh touched his. As she sat back on her heels again, she took his hand. He looked at her in surprise but smiled. "Thank you."

He laced his fingers through hers and gave her hand a gentle squeeze. "You're welcome."

They knelt there on the sand together for a few more minutes and watched the point of light in the distance. *Even if I never hold his hand like this again, it feels right.* The sky over the lake lit up with a silvery glow from tendrils of light and mist and a few streaks of rainbowed colors. Lily glanced over her shoulder at the coven around their campfire, all of whom now stood facing the lake, their arms open and their faces raised toward the sky.

"Why are you laughing?" Romeo asked.

"Mom always did this in private. I didn't know anyone else would care. We never—"

A shower of brilliant-blue and flashing-silver sparks erupted above the illuminated mist like fireworks. Although the loud music still played through their speakers, the other witches on their right had stopped their shenanigans long enough to offer their own tribute, which was as loud and flashy and inappropriate as they were.

"You said it." He chuckled.

"Said what?"

"Intention over results."

Lily shook her head. "Yeah, we can go with that."

When she looked into the combination of two contrasting covens supporting her request from the source of all magic itself, she identified a shape that took form in the mist and the colored sparks. "Does that look like anything to you?"

Tilting his head, Romeo squinted at the lights above the lake. "A giant bird."

"Yeah, that's what I thought. I'm, uh...not so sure it's supposed to do that." She looked at the smaller coven in white, who didn't notice the massive shadow of the huge avian with its wings spread wide over the lake. The partying witches paid even less attention. "Something's wrong."

"Lily, it's okay."

"No, I think..." She paused, then ran her tongue over the roof of her mouth again. "Do you smell smoke?"

"Well, there's a campfire right over there."

"Not that. It's something else." She searched wildly along the lake but there were no more black birds, no more witches in suits, and no more green fireballs. "When I woke up this morning, right after I saw the shadow in the mirror, I tasted the same thing—smoke. And magic, I think. Romeo, I don't know what's happening, but that bird"—she nodded at the smoky outline of it in the sky—"and all the others mean something."

He looked at the shimmering energy of one coven and

the sparking fireworks of the other above the lake. "Yeah, I gotta admit it doesn't sound like dreaming about Chuck E Cheese anymore. But it's not...I mean, it's not hurting anybody."

Lily squinted at the silhouette, which was almost gone now. "Not yet. If nothing else, I'd say we're definitely on the right track to find something big. The business card has the same bird on it, I think."

"The heron."

"Right. I think the guidance ritual gave us a very clear answer."

Both the white-wearing coven and the partiers went back to their own ways of celebrating Midsummer, and none of them noticed the cloud-like smoky bird over the lake. Lily and Romeo stayed there for a while longer, kneeling in the sand with their fingers intertwined. Once twilight faded into complete darkness, she slid her hand out of his and focused on the lone candle floating on the surface of the black lake. She flicked her finger and the single flame snuffed out.

"Why'd you put it out?" The coven's bonfire was larger and brighter in the darkness, illuminating Romeo's curious frown.

"Why did I put out an untended candle in the middle of a forest?"

"I mean..." Romeo looked at the dark lake again and pointed at it. "It's in the middle of a lake."

She pushed herself to her feet and brushed the damp sand off her joggers and her bare shins. "I learned my lesson when your dad let me have it for not turning down the lamp in his cousin's cabin. Do you remember that?"

"Oh, yeah." He stood too but didn't bother to brush off his sand-covered knees. "I thought you were gonna break down crying."

"But I didn't." They headed back toward the bench.

"I would've. I guess that's why I always turned the lamps down."

"Right. And why I put the candle out. Oh, and after he yelled at me that morning"—she turned to face him and walked backward across the sand—"I dragged you into the woods with me to hack at a few trees with those stupidly dull machetes."

"Yeah, that was terrifying." Romeo chuckled and rubbed the back of his neck. "I almost expected you to use me as target practice after that."

Lily spread her arms. "Hey, it was an effective outlet for processing emotions, okay? I pretended those trees were Julian Stephens."

"You didn't."

"Come on. You know I love your dad. But I'm not a fan of people screaming at me to make a point." She squinted out over the water. "At least not at the first mistake. Also, if the ritual is what churned out that bird in the smoke that no one else can see, it's probably a good idea not to let it keep going, just in case."

They sat on the bench again and Romeo sighed before he freed one more can for each of them. "This could be considered a way to settle our nerves. 'Cause I'm not sure how I feel about getting actual messages from the spirits of magic that make you taste weird things." He handed one to Lily, and they popped the tabs together. "Or we could call this another celebratory drink."

"Happy Midsummer." She held the beer toward him and he tapped his against it.

"Happy Midsummer, Lily."

They both took large sips, and after she had already gulped two mouthfuls, she spat the third onto the sand beside the bench. "Oh, my God." She swiped at her mouth with the back of a hand.

"Are you okay?"

"No. This is awful."

Romeo burst out laughing, turned the can to look smugly at it, and leaned away. His massive belch echoed around them. "Yeah, that's really bad. So much for celebrating. Or trying to forget. It would've been nice of the guidance ritual to guide us away from drinking warm PBR."

"I'm a hundred percent sure that's not how those things work."

"No, probably not." He held her gaze for long enough that her cheeks grew warm. "So, it looks like we didn't bring any trouble with us. No bird attacks but a good number of witches, though."

"And none of them are trying to kill us." Lily glanced at the two covens again to double-check. "Okay, you made a good point about relaxing. Being in the moment. You know, all my mom's puzzles and her drills about needing to constantly look closely at everything? Well, I realized I haven't turned that off in a long time."

"Sometimes, a night in the woods is simply a night in the woods, Lil."

"Hey, you haven't called me that since I was ten."

He sent her a sidelong glance and smirked. "It's nice to fall back on, right?"

"Yeah. It's cute, actually. Is it getting a little chilly to you?"

"Not really."

A tiny shiver ran through her.

"Compared to home? A little." He shrugged. "You wanna head back and call it a night? It's probably a good idea to get up early again tomorrow and keep moving."

"To Canada and Le Chapeau Magique and my mom." She nodded. "Yeah. We can turn in." She stood and retrieved her flats from where she'd dropped them in the sand beside the bench.

Romeo grabbed the last beer by the plastic ring while she slipped her sandy feet into her equally sandy shoes. "Ready?"

"Yep."

The partying witches hadn't eased their wild night even a little and now, they were louder and drunker and far more obnoxious. None of them noticed the lone witch and the werewolf heading away from the lake. But when the duo stepped off the beach and onto the dirt path, a calm, gentle voice drifted toward them. "Midsummer Blessings."

Lily turned toward the white-clad coven to see them all seated around their bonfire again, this time with drinks in hand. One of the women waved in farewell. A few others lifted their tin cups. "Midsummer Blessings," she called in response with a little wave. "And thank you."

The witches nodded at her with knowing smiles, then returned to their own celebration as the two of them stepped out of the bonfire's light down the path.

"I like them," Romeo said and swung the last beer can gently as they walked. "I don't normally like witches."

"You know, I bet they'd say the same thing about you."

When they disappeared between the trees down the path, the white pillared candle floating on the dark lake burst to life with a new flame. Long after the covens returned to their campsites for the night, the ritual candle burned. White wax dripped into the black water, and it only went out again when there was nothing left to burn.

Inside the Winnie, they poured the remainder of their open beers down the kitchen sink, and Romeo put the unopened one in the fridge. He gazed around the living area and rubbed his hands together. "So where do I get to crash?"

"Oh. Uh, well, the couch pulls out into a bed. And I know I have some extra sheets and stuff somewhere." Lily spun and scanned the cabinets built below the ceiling in an effort to remember where she'd put them.

"Don't worry about it. I'll stretch out on the couch the way it is."

"Are you sure?"

"Oh, yeah. I can sleep anywhere." He winked at her, went to the bathroom, reached inside, and pulled out a trekking backpack.

"Where did that come from?" She stared at it in bemusement.

"What, this?" He smirked. "I brought it with me."

"I didn't see you bring a backpack."

He wrinkled his nose and rubbed the back of his neck. "I stuck it in there this morning. Before I woke you up."

"You know, in some situations, that's considered a sign of trying to move in with someone—secretly stashing your stuff in the bathroom." She fisted a hand on her hip.

"Oh, but not this situation." He dropped the backpack in front of the couch. "This is only me being prepared. I'm definitely not trying to creep into your personal space."

"No, please. Feel free to creep all you want." He turned to grin at her, and she raised a finger. "I mean within reason."

"Yes, ma'am. Only reasonable creeping. Got it." He chuckled, and she stepped toward him.

"So..." Lily gazed at him, needing to speak but a little uncomfortable.

"So?" Romeo lowered his head and pressed his lips together in a smile.

"Well, thank you. For not thinking I've gone crazy over my mom. You know, believing me and coming with me. It really means a lot."

He nodded. "Good."

"Okay."

"Okay."

She took a deep breath. "Good night, then. I guess."

"Good night."

"Yeah." She bit her lip, turned hesitantly away, and

forced herself to walk toward her bedroom. When she looked back, Romeo was still watching her with that soft smile. She grinned and tucked her hair behind her ear. Her shoulder bumped against the doorway, which made her pay enough attention to slip quickly into the bedroom and slide the door closed behind her. It was hard not to slam it against the wooden trim. She puffed out a huge sigh and whispered, "Oh, my God. Why did I walk away?"

She turned and flopped backward across the side of the bed.

AFTER LYING under the covers for another hour listening to the hum of the RV's generator and the small fan she'd mounted beside the open window's screen, Lily decided she'd had enough. "This is stupid," she whispered. "Exactly like in the movies. He was obviously waiting for me to make a move. Is there some kinda secret rule I don't know about that says not to start falling for your best friend?"

She sat up in bed, tossed the covers aside, and went to the wardrobe to find something to put on. *Oversized t-shirt...where the heck did this come from—oh.* She held the gray t-shirt up and stared at the rainbow-striped Phish logo in the center. "Yeah, okay." When she'd slipped it quickly over her head, she smoothed her hair down, pulled it back, and draped it all forward over one shoulder. "Okay. Stop thinking and go tell him."

The sliding door to her room sounded too loud when

she opened it, but her bare feet were quiet across the wooden floor into the kitchen. "Romeo?" she called, her voice almost a whisper. "Are you asleep?" When she peered around the corner, she still couldn't see the couch over the two-person kitchen table. She stepped forward into the living area and froze.

"Oh, great. He's not even here." Lily glanced around the RV again like it was even possible to miss him on her way out. The bathroom door was wide open and the tiny space was empty. "So he stepped out into the night on his own." His shorts were draped over the couch's armrest and his shirt tossed onto the cushion. "As a wolf." She opened the Winnebago's side door and looked outside with no success. Disappointed, she shut it again and paused beside the couch. "Well, I guess I'll have to wait for the right time. Which probably would've been tonight. Or I've gone all bird-brained and have no idea what I— Oh, ha, ha. Bird-brained."

She rolled her eyes and glanced at Romeo's shirt one more time. Before she registered what she was doing, she stepped lightly toward the couch, snatched his shirt up, and pressed it against her nose. It smelled like him, all right —damp earth and sunbaked stone and something like cedar. It smelled like home.

"Oh, my God." She jerked the shirt away from her face and tossed it back onto the couch like it had actually bitten her. "I need to try to decipher what that black heron is about, or I need to sleep. Romeo came to help me, not to distract me." She nodded firmly, sent the couch a skeptical glare, and spun around to search the RV again, just in case.

"No, he is not hiding in the cabinets, Lily." She released a short, irritated breath, balled her hands into fists, and returned swiftly to her room. With the door closed behind her, she tried to think of anything but the smell of him until she fell asleep.

TWELVE

Disturbed by a few gentle knocks on her bedroom door, Lily jerked up in bed with a gasp.

"Lily?"

"I'm up!" she gurgled, then cleared her throat. "I'm up."

"Uh...okay—"

"Don't come in."

Romeo chuckled on the other side of the thin door. "I wasn't planning to. I only came to tell you breakfast is ready."

She scowled at the comforter still draped over her legs. "Aw, you made me breakfast? Wait, is that bacon again?"

"Yep."

"I'll be out in a sec."

"Don't let it get cold."

She glanced at the door. "Blasphemy. How could you say such a thing?"

The sound of his chuckle faded as he went back into the tiny kitchen to tend to breakfast.

Lily eyed the gray Phish t-shirt on the floor, bundled it up hastily before she stuffed it into her wardrobe, and searched for something a little more presentable. Her stomach emitted a ferocious growl at the smell of bacon. "I'm not sure if the Winnie smelling like bacon for the next few weeks is gonna be amazing or disappointing. I suppose I'll always need bacon, now." With a sigh, she snatched up a lacey cream top with sleeves cut directly below the shoulder and a pair of dark-green capris.

She dressed, looked at herself in the mirror on the wardrobe door, and ran her finger through her hair. Finally, she shrugged. "You're allowed to look like you just woke up."

The aroma of freshly cooked bacon struck her like a smack to the face by the god of bacon's right hand. "There is literally nothing better than waking up to that." Her stomach rumbled again.

"Oh, hey." Romeo stepped back from the stove, the tongs in one hand, a plate of crispy bacon in the other, and no shirt. "I actually thought you'd take longer to come out. You look nice."

She almost laughed. "Well, thanks. Uh...so do you." It was hard to keep from staring at his bare chest, his chiseled shoulder, and the way his left bicep flexed simply from holding the plate of bacon. "You're making yourself at home. That's good. Do you always cook bacon shirtless?"

"What?" He jerked his head down to look at himself like he'd forgotten he hadn't put on a shirt. That simple action flexed his abs, and she glanced quickly at the other side of the RV as she smoothed her hair away from her face. He shrugged and went back to plating the rest of the bacon. "I went for a run this morning."

"Also shirtless?" Lily smirked and spared him another glance.

He tipped his head back. "No. I took off a really sweaty shirt and...wanted to make you breakfast first before I showered." His grin was appealing. "I didn't want to make you wait on me."

"A thousand thank yous, breakfast master."

Romeo bowed like he was on stage before he moved toward the small table nestled between the tiny stall of a bathroom and the couch. It was already set with a plate of still-steaming eggs and two bananas. He set the bacon down, turned to face her, and gestured with an open hand. "Care to join me?"

She laughed. "Fruit."

"Bananas."

"You really stepped it up with adding another food group."

"Thank you. I'm trying. Oh." He grabbed one of the mugs sitting on the table. "It's not a real breakfast without coffee."

"No, it's not." When he handed her the mug, she wrapped both hands around it and stared at him. "Did you bring coffee?"

"Yep. I used your French press."

"I...don't have a French press."

When he leaned sideways across the narrow kitchen

toward the counter, Lily's eyes went instantly to that perfect v-cut of his lower abs that dipped beneath the waistband of his shorts. She took a long, slow slurp to distract herself and didn't taste a thing.

"If you've used this thing for something not coffee-related," he said as he hooked one finger through the sixteen-ounce press' metal handle and lifted it, "I would really like to hear what that is."

She tilted her head in confusion. "Where did you find that?"

"In your cabinet."

"Huh." Her gaze flickered around the Winnie's kitchen before a chuckle spilled out of her. "I've budgeted for Starbucks every morning and I never even thought to look for a coffeemaker."

"You know, you can buy everything you need to make a good cup of coffee at the store." He tried not to laugh at her.

"Yes, I realize this. Now." Lily grinned at him as she slid into the booth at the table. "There are many things I never had to think about before—I mean, before I had no money and had to start thinking about them." She shrugged. "Thank you for the wakeup call."

"No problem." He sat across from her, his knees sliding along the underside of the table not built for someone his height, and grabbed the other mug. "I hope you don't mind that I used the rest of your milk."

"You made me coffee and bacon. You can basically do whatever you want now."

Romeo pointed at her. "I'm gonna hold you to that.

Coffee would've been better with whole milk, though. Or half-and-half."

"How 'bout after we find whatever my mom wanted me to see in Montreal, we go grocery shopping? Stock the fridge. And I'll let you walk me through all the things I've apparently forgotten a grown person can buy for a Winnebago. DIY adulting."

He snorted and nodded. "Consider me your guide through the breakfast and kitchenware aisles."

She blew across the top of the coffee, and her next sip warmed her all the way down to her toes. Her eyes fluttered closed.

"Eggs?"

Lily eyed the serving spoon and the huge helping of scrambled eggs with green onion mixed in. Her stomach growled again. "Yeah. Definitely."

He shook his head and laughed as he served her a heaping pile of eggs, followed by four strips of bacon. With a smile, he lifted his mug toward her, nodded, and dug into his breakfast like he hadn't eaten solid food in a week. "Hey, did you go through my clothes last night?"

She paused with a forkful of food halfway to her mouth before she shoved it in and swallowed quickly. "No. I mean, I couldn't sleep last night, so I came out to see if you were up. I definitely didn't go through your clothes." *That's not technically a lie.* "Did you have a nice little jaunt out there after dark?"

"Yep." He took another bite of his bacon and looked frankly at her. "It helps to clear my head a little."

"Why'd you need to clear your head?"

"Why couldn't you sleep?"

Lily raised an eyebrow and smirked at him over the rim of her mug. "I'll tell you mine if you tell me yours."

"Hmm." Romeo squinted at her before he took a deep breath and crammed his mouth with more bacon. "Maybe later. We're focusing on following your mom's clues and finding out what they mean. I definitely don't want to distract you."

"You know virtually everything that's going on with me at this point." She set her coffee down. "Seriously, Romeo, if something's going on, you can tell me."

"I know. I will. Just...later." He took a long sip and looked speculatively at her. "I could've sworn I smelled you on my clothes last night, though."

"You can smell me?"

"Well, yeah. I could pick out your scent three miles away from across a crowded—" He stopped abruptly and cleared his throat. "Yes. Everyone has their own smell."

"I see." *And what would've happened if I came out of my room last night before he went wolfing through the forest?*

"How're the eggs?"

"Perfectly eggy, thank you."

"Good."

AFTER THEY'D WASHED ALL the dishes and dried them to his surprisingly high standards of cleanliness, she caught him sniffing covertly at his armpit. He jerked his head away and snorted in disgust. "Uh...did you fill the water tank when we got here?"

Lily pressed her lips together and tried not to laugh. He'd gone from werewolf to Wookie and couldn't handle the smell. "Yep. I showed you that part too when we hooked up, remember?"

Romeo looked at her with wide eyes, suddenly aware of the small space in the Winnebago and how close they'd been all morning. "Sorry about...I mean, I should've—" He sighed and nodded. "I'm gonna take that shower now." He knelt beside his pack, pulled out a few fresh clothes, and smiled like it hurt. "Are there towels in the bathroom?"

"Uh..." Lily's gaze flickered toward the tiny stall with its cramped toilet, shallow sink, and one-person shower. "They have showers here. Right outside. Anything has to be bigger than what I've got."

"If you have water and towels, I'm good." Putting as much distance between them as he could, he shuffled around her and slipped through the bathroom doorway.

"I really think you'd like the campsite's showers far more," she added and tried not to sound too concerned about it.

"This is fine." He pulled the narrow door shut.

"Okay, but I should probably warn you—"

He opened the door again enough for him to press his face through the opening. "You do have soap, right?"

"Of course I have soap. That's not what I'm trying to—"

The door snapped closed again. "Okay, great. Thanks. I'll be fast." His urgent dismissal was muffled through the door, and before Lily could get in another word, the shower turned on.

"I hope you mean faster than four and a half minutes 'cause you're about to find out why I showered at your place." Of course, he didn't hear her. Lily retrieved her phone from her purse in the center console and flopped down on the couch to wait, strangely aware of the fact that he'd slept in that very place last night. She lit the phone's screen up to time the shower. "I cast the spell to try to fix it. Maybe the shower only screws around with me." When she saw the time on her phone, she laughed. "It does not feel like seven in the morning right now. I'm normally way grumpier than this."

At exactly four and a half minutes, the shower shut off, abruptly followed by, "What the—" The faucet handles squeaked a little as Romeo fiddled with them. He pounded on the shower stall a few times. "Uh, Lily?"

"Yep. I got it." She stood from the couch and dropped her phone back into her purse. "Remember that'll keep happening, okay? So...sorry." His only response was a deep sigh before she stepped outside to the water tank's access panel on the side of the RV. Her cheeks burned in a high flush as she opened the panel, unscrewed the cap to the water tank, and screwed it back on again. That was the only way she'd found to undo her irritating mistake with the ridiculously short showers. The water pumped through the RV's system again, and she took a deep breath.

The other two RVs hooked up at the sites on either side of her were far enough away that she didn't feel like she was intruding. One of the women from the white-clad coven the night before sat in front of the closest motorhome. She nursed a mug of something and wore pajama pants and an oversized t-shirt now instead of flowing white linens. From her chair beneath the RV's awning, she raised a hand and greeted Lily with a friendly grin, who returned the gesture before she made her way back inside. "I assume the party witches brought tents. Or passed out at the lake."

She had enough time to pull her hair back into a ponytail before the shower turned off again. Lily sat in the armchair mounted behind the front passenger seat and crossed her legs. Romeo growled and muttered something in the bathroom, then stepped out a few minutes later in baby-blue shorts and a slate-gray t-shirt, his hair still dripping wet.

"What's the deal with your shower?" he asked and gestured behind him with a thumb before he shoved his dirty clothes into his pack.

She tucked her hair behind her ear and smiled at the Winnie's beige carpeting. "I tried to fix it, honestly."

"What was it like before that?"

"Well, I only tried to change the water. You know, when it's all soft and slimy and you can't wash anything off?"

"Yeah, like at the cabin." He tousled his hair.

"I thought I could set the tank so no matter what water I hooked up to, it wouldn't come out like that. Admittedly, that part actually worked, but now I'm down to four-and-a-half-minute showers, and I'm not quite sure how to undo whatever timer I put on it."

He looked at her with a stupefied expression. "I find it hard to believe that you don't know how to undo a spell."

"Yeah, and it's a little embarrassing." Lily shrugged. "I'm sure there's a category of magic specifically for plumbing, but that's not really my area of expertise."

He laughed and shook his head. "I bet you've become really good at taking super-fast showers."

"Not really. It's more like getting good at braving the elements and whoever happens to see me running out to the water covered in soap. Not my proudest moment of self-sufficiency."

"Huh." His blank expression morphed into a grin. "Now that's something I'd like to see."

"Yeah, I bet it is. Hey, but you can't say I didn't try to warn you."

"Actually, you suggested the campsite showers."

"Okay, next time, I'll shout exactly what I mean, loud and clear. And I promise there are no more surprises as far as the plumbing goes."

Laughing, he stood and headed toward the front of the Winnie. "Good to know. Hey, if we leave right now, we can beat the traffic and maybe even avoid a backup at the border—" His eyes widened, and he whirled to launch himself toward his pack beside the couch.

"What's wrong?"

He scrabbled through his belongings and tossed aside clothes, two books, a stackable set of plastic dinnerware, and two toothbrushes. Finally, he withdrew the telltale navy book of his passport and jerked the cover open. "Shit."

"What's wrong?"

When he looked at her, his neck had taken on a blotchy redness. "I didn't even think about it. I was excited to get going with you, trying to get everything ready, and I—"

"Hey, it's okay." Lily stood from the armchair to kneel beside him on the carpet. "Whatever it is, we can fix it."

Romeo clenched his eyes shut tightly and puffed out a breath. "It's so stupid."

"Maybe. We can hold off the judgment until you tell me what's going on."

"My passport's expired."

She winced. "Oh."

"I'm so sorry. I can order one from wherever we are, but it's gonna slow us down. And I didn't wanna have to—"

"Wait a minute. Slow down." She put a hand on his shoulder and squeezed it before she released it. "You're beating yourself up for no reason. This is a super-easy fix."

"Lily, you can't wait around for me to get a new passport. You can drop me off in Syracuse. I'll think of something or maybe join you later—"

"What? No way. I need my navigator and sidekick-slash-DJ." She smiled at him and nodded. "And I'm not gonna let a little technical detail stop us. Can I see?"

He handed the passport to her and sighed again as he shook his head. "What are our options?"

She winked. "Don't forget, your best friend's a witch. Okay, to be clear, I wouldn't do this if we were on a normal road trip. But it's my mom we're talking about. A little magic to follow the law never hurt anybody, right?" She blew lightly on the tip of her finger, pressed it to the expiration date of the passport, and completed the glamor spell. The last two digits of the year slowly melted away to be replaced by those for two years into the future and she grinned. "There. I can't do this all the time so we'll have to find somewhere to update this for real, but—" She turned to look at him and found his face barely inches from hers as he leaned toward her to study his passport. Her gaze dropped to his lips.

Romeo took the passport. A tiny smile flickered at the corner of his mouth. With a sharp breath, he leaned away from her to sit on the floor of the RV and cross his legs beneath him. Lily swallowed. "Are you sure that'll work?" he asked.

"For the next twenty-four hours, absolutely. Okay, you look skeptical, so let me add that I did this a few times in high school. Not with passports, but with my driver's license."

"You forged your own fake ID."

"Yes. And it was only a few times. It was also stupid and reckless, and the clubs I got into were never as much fun as I thought they'd be. Let's move past that part, shall we? I think this counts as an unselfish reason to change a few dates."

"Yeah. To go find your mom."

"Right. So I suggest we don't take twenty-four hours to get from here to the border. And when we get there, act like we're not trying to get away with something. Do you think you can do that?" Romeo took a deep breath. "You can order a new passport when we have a little downtime. And I promise everything will be fine. I gotcha."

"Yeah...yeah, okay." He stuffed everything he'd tossed out of his pack into it again, stared at his passport one more time, and tucked that away too. "Do you want me to drive this round? Let you relax a little."

"This is me being completely honest right now. You look too nervous to drive."

"No, I don't."

"Well, either you're sweating, or your hair's still wet." Lily snorted.

"Um..." He wiped his forehead and ran his hand through his damp curls. "That's water."

"Well, good." She laughed and stood from the floor. "Still, I'm gonna drive today. I would feel better about letting you behind the wheel if you wanted to come learn how to unhook everything from the campsite." She headed toward the RV's side door.

"Oh, I see. This is a Winnebago Adventurer Operator's Test, right?"

She looked at him over her shoulder and grinned. "This is only the beginning, young grasshopper."

THIRTEEN

After an hour back on I-81, Lily began to regret not letting him drive. Her record of hours driven in twenty-four hours was about eight, and this was more than twice that. Thankfully, she still had one energy drink left and she didn't hesitate to open it to keep her spirits up.

It turned out to be another beautiful, sunny day driving through the Pennsylvania countryside, which felt weirdly nostalgic until they reached Scranton. It wasn't Charleston or New York or Boston, but it was at least a city. "Okay, this might sound kinda weird, but after spending a night in the woods, even a city this size feels too crowded."

"It's not weird at all." Romeo slumped in the passenger seat. "Do you know what we need?" he asked.

"Judging by that crazy smile, I assume it's something awesome." She tried to hold her laughter back and focus on the road at the same time.

"Assuming that our definitions of awesome are still the same."

"All right. So what do we need right now?"

"A theme song."

She snorted and adjusted her grip on the steering wheel. "What?"

"Yep. Something that screams, 'witch and werewolf super-team off to find hidden clues and—'" He frowned in thought for a moment. "Well, your mom."

"Okay, I dare you to find a song already in existence that checks all those boxes."

"Challenge accepted." With his phone plugged into the RV's stereo, he pulled up the first song she hadn't heard in ages—drums, guitar, and finally, the harmonica came in.

"'Life is a Highway?'"

"Hey, it's fitting, right? Come on, try it."

They listened to the entire song, and Lily even joined in with Tom Cochrane on the chorus. When it was over, Romeo turned to her and wiggled his eyebrows. "I'm not quite feeling it." She shook her head. "Let's try something else."

They went through Red Hot Chili Peppers, The Eagles, Grateful Dead, Steppenwolf, Tom Petty, Bruce Springsteen, and something she made him switch immediately because it sounded like a number of songs playing at the same time—all of them about road trips or traveling or running free. "You have a seriously weird music collection," she said and tried to look at him a second at a time so she didn't steer them off the road. "You know that, right?"

"Now who's the young grasshopper? We'll find that

theme song. Just wait." Romeo scrolled through his phone and burst out laughing. "Let's go with something different, huh?" As soon as he pressed play, a flurry of notes from a flute and a piccolo filled the RV. When the first line of lyrics—"Lend me your ear while I call you a fool"—rose through the speakers, Lily's mouth dropped open in a mix of surprise and confusion.

"What is this?"

"Jethro Tull, baby. 'The Witch's Promise!'" He grinned at her and nodded his head to the beat.

"I feel like we stepped into a Renaissance Festival. Do you hear these lyrics?"

"Hey, loosen up, Lil. Let DJ Romeo make this a truly magical experience for you."

"More DJ Pun Master." She swallowed another huge mouthful of energy drink.

"Hey, that name might actually stick. I could go places with that one." They shared a look and cracked up before he turned the volume up to concert-level decibels.

IN NEW YORK, they pulled off the highway two more times. The first stop was to use the facilities and stock up on necessities like more Red Bulls, beef jerky, Snickers, and the only snack food Lily had let herself eat on a regular basis since she was fourteen, which happened to be cheddar popcorn. The second stop two hours later was for lunch in Watertown, about half an hour from the Canadian border. They bought sandwiches at the gas station, and she gave him the second half of hers without saying she couldn't handle the rest of it with all that mayo and soggy bread. He didn't taste the difference.

Romeo retrieved his passport from his pack, and Lily made sure to pull hers out of the drawer of random things in the kitchen before they headed to the border crossing at Thousand Islands Bridge. Lucky for them, they beat the traffic on I-81 into Canada, and the Winnebago slowed behind four other cars lined up at the port. When they were down to two cars in front of them, he began to fiddle with his passport—flipped through the pages, bent it and straightened it a few times, and let it fall open in his hands before he slapped it shut in constant distraction.

"Hey," Lily said gently, "remember when I said to act like we're not trying to get away with something?" He sniffed and stared at the US document in his lap. "This is the perfect time to do that."

"Are you sure this is gonna work?"

"Completely sure. As long as the customs officers don't try to look you up in the system, we'll be fine."

He sighed and chewed on the inside of his cheek. "Yeah, but I think they do that."

"What?"

"I think that's part of the process. I've already been to jail once, Lily. The last thing I need is to go back there."

"Hey." She turned in the driver's seat to face him and waited for him to look at her. "Do you trust me?"

"Yeah."

"Good. Nothing will happen. And if by some crazy,

inexplicable reason it does, I'll make sure we both get out of it in one piece. I promise."

Dropping his head back against the headrest, Romeo closed his eyes and puffed out a massive breath. "We're doing this for Greta."

"We're doing it for Greta. The sooner we find her, the sooner we can go home and pick up where we left off." He shot her a glance, and Lily shrugged. "Okay, maybe not right where we left off. I really like having you around again."

"Yeah. Me too."

"So can you please stop ripping your passport up and take a deep breath? Maybe meditate?"

"Meditate?"

Ten minutes later, Lily already had her window rolled completely down when she pulled up to the next open customs booth at the border crossing. "Hi. How are you?" She smiled sweetly and leaned against the door.

The customs officer smiled but he looked tired and a little bored, which was only fair. "Fine, thank you. Documents, please." She took Romeo's when he offered it, sent him a quick wink, and stacked it beneath hers before she handed them through the window. The man scanned hers first, looked at her, and shuffled it under the other before he studied that one for a few seconds longer. When he looked up again, he leaned sideways to peer past her, and Romeo raised a hand for a weak wave. "What brings you to Canada?"

"We're coming to see Montreal," Lily said. "We've

heard about how awesome it is and finally decided to see for ourselves."

The man wrote down her answers on a little pad, checked off boxes, or quoted her verbatim for legal posterity. "How long do you plan to stay?"

"This is our big summer vacation. We'll spend a few nights in some of your excellent Canadian campgrounds we've heard so much about." She patted the steering wheel. "We won't be any longer than next weekend before getting back to the daily grind."

"Do you have any family in the country?"

"Nope."

"Will your vehicle or anything inside it be used for any business-related purposes, including the sale or distribution of any items you bring with you into Canada?"

"Nope." She grinned. "This trip is purely for pleasure."

That made the officer look up from his checklist and directly into her eyes. His narrowed a little, and she managed not to react although the grin felt frozen on her face. He returned his gaze to the clipboard. "Any animals inside the vehicle?"

Lily almost turned to glance at Romeo but held the impulse back. "No."

"Produce or uncooked meat?"

"We only have camping food. Cooked sausage and some baked beans left. Potato salad. Definitely no produce. Are those gonna be an issue?"

"Shouldn't be. I'll run your information through the system now. It only takes a few minutes."

"Of course."

"Just a minute."

Romeo started to cough and snatched up the energy drink Lily had opened on this trip. He chugged the rest of it in seconds.

"Hey, I'm not sure that's the best idea if you're trying not to look nervous," she whispered.

"But it's something."

She eyed the retreating customs officer casually with a smile. "You were right. He's running us through the system. I'm fairly sure an echo spell would work and make sure that what he sees on his computer copies what he saw on your passport—what is that?"

"What?" Romeo leaned forward to look through the driver's side window.

"No, um..." She patted his arm and gestured directly ahead. The air immediately beyond the checkpoint shimmered with a silver-green light. "You see that, right?"

"Yeah." He swallowed. "Do they?"

"I seriously doubt it. All the magicals I know prefer jobs with a little more independence, not border security. And border laws don't really apply in the same way on the northern border. So why is there a spell wall hidden from non-magicals right on the line between—oh, no."

"Lily?"

"Please tell me you don't see that and it's only another vision coming at me, so I don't have to do something reckless right now to save somebody's life." She took a deep breath and stared through the windshield.

"If you're talking about that giant bird-looking thing on

the other side of that shimmering light...uh, no. I wouldn't call that a vision."

"No, no, no. Please go away." She swatted uselessly without realizing she'd raised her hand.

"Do you know how to stop it?"

"I don't even know what it is."

The massive black shadow swooped toward the spell wall, its wings spanning a dozen feet across. The shimmering light flashed a dark, sickly green and cast an eerie glow over Lily and Romeo's face when the bird shadow broke through to the US side. It shrank into a single point of darkness and darted toward the custom's officer with their passports.

"No, no!" Lily shoved her hand through the window and pointed at the officer, ready to put a shield around him now that the thing following her had decided to attack innocent non-magicals. "Watch out!"

But the streak of black shadow missed the officer altogether and darted into the device with which he was about to scan Romeo's passport. The man looked at her and frowned.

"Sorry." She shrugged and offered him a sheepish smile. "There was a...wasp."

"A huge wasp," Romeo echoed through the window.

"I'm allergic."

Without emotion, the official returned his attention to the scanner before he returned it through the booth window.

"That was some quick thinking," Romeo muttered.

"It could've been better, but thank you. Now, I'd really like to know what all that was about."

The custom's officer approached Lily's window again and blandly handed her the passports. "There are a lot of wasps up here," he said. "Especially if you're going camping. If you have an EpiPen or allergy mediation, I hope you brought it with you."

She patted her purse and grinned. "I never leave home without it."

He studied her for a moment before he nodded. "If you had a smaller car and a trunk, I'd ask you to open it for me. But with the RV, I'll need to step aboard your vehicle and take a look around. That all right with you?" He leaned over again to meet Romeo's gaze.

"Come on in," Romeo replied and swung his arm in a gesture that would've been welcoming if it wasn't so wildly exaggerated. "We have nothing to hide."

The officer nodded in appreciation of the extra effort and said, "Can you open the door for me when I walk around?"

"No problem." She stood from her seat and leaned toward Romeo. "Stay there and don't say anything else. Please. I got this." He sighed and leaned back in the seat but he took her request to heart and didn't try to argue.

AFTER THE OFFICER cleared them to pass, Lily moved forward slowly toward the series of bridges connecting all the islands that made up Thousand Islands Bridge. When they drove through the wall of silver-green magic, a breeze came out of nowhere and ruffled her hair.

"Okay, that felt like walking under those super annoying fans at the grocery store."

"What?"

"You know. The ones hanging over the front doors. Is your window up?"

"All the way."

"Mine too. So that little puff of air came from whatever magic we drove through." She glanced in her side mirrors. The spell wall was still there, shimmering like a mirage. "At least the shadow hasn't made another appearance."

"You know those fans at the stores are to keep the bugs out, right?"

"For real?"

Romeo chuckled. "What did you think they were for?"

"I...I don't know. To cool you off before you step into the AC? But the bug thing makes way more sense."

"Yes. Yes, it does."

"We're not bugs, though."

"Lily, I hate to say I'm not following your train of thought right now."

"I simply mean..." She checked the side mirror again but saw no shadow, no witches, and no giant bird. "What if that wall does essentially the same thing?"

"I have a feeling you're not talking about keeping American bugs out of Canada."

She scrunched her face up and cut off a laugh. "No. I mean what if someone cast it there to keep certain people from crossing the border? Certain magicals?"

"You did say border laws don't apply in the same way—"

"I know. But we went right through too easily. So if the wall's keeping someone out, that means it's not trying to keep me from my mom. In theory, right?"

"Yeah..."

"And that bird shadow went directly to the officer's passport scanner. Nothing else." She slammed her hand down on the steering wheel. "Holy crap!"

"Okay. You're brainstorming. I can wait."

"Sorry. I only—" She looked at him and her whole face lit up in realization. "I'm starting to think maybe that bird shadow isn't trying to attack me. Maybe it's trying to help me instead."

"So you don't think it's connected to the witch who came after you?"

"I only know that I saw them both the same day—at your house before we left yesterday. First, the shadow in my mirror, then the witch running down the street. But that time, it wasn't real."

"Yeah, looking at it that way, it sounds like someone's trying to send you a message."

"Yes." Lily's grin fell into a frown. "Now I have to find out who it is and what the heck they're trying to say."

"Well, there's a black bird on that business card." Romeo nodded at her purse. "You know, I wasn't entirely sure that's where we needed to go until right now."

"I'm glad you're convinced. Officially."

"Officially, yeah. How do you think your mom's connected to the black heron?"

She shook her head. "I haven't figured that one out yet. But we're about to find out." Pushing herself straighter against the back of the seat, she flexed her fingers before she grasped the steering wheel again. "Music?"

"Yeah." He retrieved his phone, tapped absently at the screen, and dropped it into the cupholder. The music came through loud and clear—a great guitar opening, a pleasant bluesy feel, and when Dan Auerbach's voice rose above it all, Lily smiled.

"Yes. We can definitely agree on The Black Keys." It only occurred to her which song it was when the lyrics started. "Well the crooks are out / And the streets are gray..." She pressed her lips together and held her breath. "Did you pick this song on purpose, or—"

"It's on shuffle," he said flatly and stared out the windshield with no expression whatsoever. A second later, he turned toward her and smirked.

"Boy with a broken halo, huh?"

"That's me."

"You're not as bad as you think."

FOURTEEN

The remainder of the drive took them along the northern bank of the St. Lawrence River. At about 3:00 p.m. the ON-401 brought them to Rue Saint-Antoine O and into the heart of Montreal, Quebec. Sunlight glinted off the river, gulls swooped and shrieked at each other, and a collection of glittering skyscrapers rose in front of them. "This is not what I expected of Canada," Lily muttered and ducked on reflex to get a better view despite the Winnie's massive windshield. Everything was so bright, and the city was much bigger than she'd expected.

"It could almost be Charleston if you took out all the skyscrapers," Romeo commented. "And turned the river into the ocean."

"Don't let your dad hear you say that."

He snorted and picked his phone up. "So. Parking garage... It looks like there's a decent one for larger vehicles on Stanley Street. I'm reasonably sure we can get anywhere we need to be from there."

"Yeah, that actually sounds like Charleston too. Take us there, navigator."

The traffic also echoed their hometown with narrow streets clogged with cars and buses, pedestrians everywhere, and college students milling around in droves as they enjoyed the height of their summer. "One more tourist destination. They even have a port and everything. This is like driving down Meeting Street." She blinked away the déjà vu. "Except they traded assassin witches for skyscrapers."

Romeo made it easy to navigate through the streets until they reached the parking garage. "Is it weird that I'm comforted by the fact that Canada doesn't build their garages much differently than ours?" he asked.

"It's not weird. I feel it too." Lily's memories made her chuckle. "Mom always said traveling opened her eyes to new possibilities, even with as much as she traveled. Maybe this was what she meant."

The payment system was a little different at the kiosk. "You speak French, right?" Romeo nodded at the scrolling letters.

"Yes. I do. And for your benefit, we'll switch to English."

"Oh, my benefit, huh?" He lowered his head. "Yeah, I appreciate it."

"Okay. All paid up. Let's do this." They set out onto Montreal's sidewalks lining the wide streets.

"Wait a minute." He stopped to look at his phone and Lily simply gazed at the people, the sunshine reflected off the water, and the glistening storefronts in every direction. "Le Chapeau Magique doesn't open until five thirty. So we have a little time to kill—hey."

"Huh?" Lily's neck was craned almost all the way back as her gaze followed the impressive rise of buildings taller than she'd seen in a long time.

"Is the big city blowing your mind right now?"

"What?" When she jerked her head to look at him, he chuckled quietly, his green eyes alive and expectant. "Only the buildings. The last time I was in New York was that Phish show with my mom. And I didn't really leave Charleston much after that. She was the one who liked to bounce around. I can handle a city."

"I know. I wanted to check and make sure you were paying attention because I found something we could do for the next two hours."

"Okay." She turned fully toward him and nodded. "Let's hear it."

With a fist pressed to his mouth, he made a big show of clearing his throat. "Care to join me for a walk along the promenade?" He stuck out his elbow to offer her his arm.

Lily's laughter made him grin. "What was that accent supposed to be?"

"Uh...the kind that'll get you to say yes?"

"Hey, good answer." She raised an eyebrow and shot him a coy smile before she slid her arm through his. "What's this promenade, then?"

"Promenade du Vieux-Port."

"Ah, le Promenade du Vieux-Port. Mais oui, bien sûr."

"I have no idea what you just said."

She tugged on his arm. "Let's go."

They set off with a fanciful strut toward the water and the Old Montreal Port. Laughing, they quickly had to give it up because the Promenade du Vieux-Port was actually a twenty-minute walk through the city and the people and the traffic. "Just 'cause I can't keep walking this slow on purpose," Romeo said.

"Uh-huh. Well, you walk however you need to walk, okay?" She loosened her hold on his arm but neither of them pulled away.

"Okay, you definitely made the right choice." Lily stared at the walkway spanning Montreal's harbor along the St. Lawrence River. "It feels like stepping into our own private park."

"Totally. Private park with hundreds of cars on the street and all these tourists."

"Plus the people who live here and get to enjoy the view. Quite the private place." She grinned at him, and they walked together with the sun behind them to cast their growing shadows across the cement and over the side of the bridge into the water.

Three seagulls dived toward them out of nowhere, squabbling over someone else's dropped potato chips. She startled and grabbed Romeo's arm with both hands to steady herself. "Oh, my God."

"I get it. Birds are creepy. And you have every reason

to be a little jumpier around them than most people." He chuckled and guided her gently into standing upright like a person who wasn't terrified of all birds.

"Seagulls are not herons." Lily cleared her throat. "And not shadows. I'm fine."

"And nothing to worry about if that shadow is actually trying to help you. Remember?"

She looked at him and studied his open expression. "I would've reasoned that out for myself, you know. But I actually really like hearing you say it out loud for me."

"Anytime. Are you good?"

She exhaled a sharp sigh and blew a few mussed strands of hair out of her face. "Totally good."

Romeo smoothed the hair from her face and eased a few stray strands from the corner of her mouth. "I actually really like being the person who knows what you're gonna tell yourself before you think it."

Lily licked her lips and held his gaze for a few more seconds. "Yeah. That too."

They resumed their walk and passed two joggers who nodded at them like they all belonged there. "Did you ever try jogging?" he asked.

"Do you mean like to help me think? I've thought about it now and then. It probably would've helped back home when I was trying to find someone who believed me—what? Why do you look like you're about to explode?"

"Uh..."

"Spit it out."

"No, I only—" Romeo shrugged, smirked at the sidewalk, and looked up at the sky. "Okay, I pictured you running in that outfit."

Lily laughed and turned to glance at the joggers who'd passed them. "Oh, yeah. Very flattering."

"You're welcome?"

"No, Romeo, I meant the tight pants."

"Right."

She leaned playfully into him to smack his chest, and the next thing she knew, she'd linked her arm even tighter in his and reached up to grab his bicep.

He shoved his free hand into the pocket of his shorts and let her keep her hand there. "A good run always helps me," he said, tipped his head back, and stared ahead down the promenade. "With the thinking part."

"Is that why you took a little trip by yourself last night?"

"Yeah...you weren't supposed to know I snuck out."

"Hey, you don't ever have to sneak out around me. You gotta do what you gotta do. You did..."

"I did what?"

She bit her lip. "Okay, you shifted first, right? I saw all your clothes on the floor, and I know that's part of it. But I wasn't sure..."

"Lily, are you trying to ask me if I streaked through the woods buck-naked on Midsummer night?"

Her mouth dropped open before she closed it hastily. "You know, yes. That's exactly what I'm asking."

"I was only naked until I stepped outside." He smirked at her.

"Well, I appreciate an honest answer."

Romeo laughed and shook his head. "That's all you'll ever get from me. You know that, right?"

"Of course I do. So why wasn't I supposed to know?"

He drew his hand from his pocket to scratch behind his ear. "I didn't want you to think that I wanted to get away from you or anything."

She squeezed his arm. "Hey, it's kinda hard to think that when you volunteered yourself to come with me. In an RV. To Canada."

"True."

"And you seemed really excited about sleeping on the couch." Lily shrugged and gazed out over the water. "I guess I assumed you didn't want to—"

"Woah, woah, woah!" He stepped sideways across the path, wrapped his arm around her, and pulled her even closer against his chest.

"What?" She looked over her shoulder to see they'd narrowly avoided being run down by a swerving ten-year-old on rollerblades being pulled at dangerous speeds by the massive golden retriever at the other end of the leash.

"Barkley, heel," the boy shouted, followed by a shriek of, "Look out!" directed at two women who had stopped in animated conversation on the walkway.

She jerked her head toward the water and sent an energetic push against one woman's back. The hapless gossiper wearing running clothes and flipflops stumbled forward against her friend with a cry of surprise a split second before the boy's runaway dog would have sent its owner crashing into her. Both women shouted after him in

French, and the boy released the leash with one hand to turn back toward them and wave. "Sorry!"

"Wow," Romeo said and stared as the kid and his dog barreled down the promenade.

"I know." Lily dragged in a breath, very much aware of the fact that he still pressed her against him with a hand on her lower back. She dared herself to look at him.

"Who names their dog Barkley?"

With a hiss of laughter, she pushed him away and resumed the walk.

"I'm serious." He chuckled and caught up to her. "There's only one pet name I know of that was worse. Do you remember Mrs. Hutchinson? She lived on the next property over from where my dad's cousin had his cabin."

"She was literally a cat lady, wasn't she?"

"The summer after sophomore year, she picked up a fat old cat from...somewhere. She told me she'd decided to call him Puss 'n Cutes."

"No."

"The thing looked miserable." Lily shook her head, and Romeo sniggered. "I think I might've chased it off into the woods one night. When I...you know." He frowned a little.

"Instincts, huh?"

"Something like that. Hey, well done with the non-jogging jogger."

She leaned away from him and smiled at the cement. "If I can't save somebody from being mauled by a happy dog, what's the point of magic?"

"You might be the only witch I know who thinks about

it that way." He bumped her shoulder with his arm, both hands already back in his pockets now.

"I'm the only witch you know, period. Besides my mom."

"Right. Well, that too."

FIFTEEN

When Lily remembered to check the time, it was already 5:00 p.m. They turned quickly and retraced their steps along the promenade toward the center of Montreal.

"Good thing Le Chapeau Magique is a restaurant," she said when they crossed the third busy street during rush-hour traffic. "I'm starving."

"You have no idea how cool it is to hear a girl admit that."

"Oh, yeah. When it's the right kinda food, I can definitely eat. And with a slogan like, 'Taste your wildest dreams,' I have a feeling we won't be disappointed." She pulled up the address for Le Chapeau Magique on her phone and sent it to her GPS. They were only fifteen minutes away and headed in the right direction. Once they turned onto Crescent Street from Saint-Catherine Street W, she felt like she'd stepped back into Charleston's East Bay Street all over again. Old stone buildings stood only two or three stories tall, one after the other in a row and separated by narrow alleyways. There were as many people there, too, hopping from bar to bar like they did back home, and they almost missed Le Chapeau Magique altogether.

"Wait, hold on." Lily turned back down the sidewalk and stopped. "That's gotta be it."

"Woah. I thought that was another alley." The front door was squashed between a bistro lounge called Thursday's and the slightly darker atmosphere of the Sir Winston Churchill Pub. The restaurant they were looking for was the only one in this strip of bars that didn't have windows facing the street.

"I think that's the point." Lily studied the narrow door painted black.

"But there's no name." Romeo gazed up at the walls and peered closer.

"Nope. Only the Order of North's sigil." A purple circle with the crescent moon and diamonds adorned the otherwise blank door. "Wait, does that look like a bird to you?" She pointed to the slightly darker outline of the same heron shape as on the business card, its wings outstretched.

"Maybe."

She looked closer. "Or I'm simply seeing birds in old paint, now. We might as well give it a try."

He pushed on the door which was too narrow for them to walk through together. She almost fell down the steep, narrow stairway leading underground immediately behind the entrance. Lanterns hanging every few feet on the walls cast a deep purple light barely bright enough to see the next stair in front of her.

"Careful," she said, turning briefly toward Romeo. "There's literally a step right when you walk in." When he closed the door behind him and shut out the daylight on Crescent Street, they stood in almost complete darkness.

"Man, for a place promising the taste of dreams, they sure make it ridiculously hard to find," Romeo muttered.

"I think it's one of those—what?" She'd reached out with both hands to steady herself against the stone walls but quickly jerked her hands back. "You know, I think damp stone walls in the dark aren't a normal indicator of a great restaurant. Or it's part of the disguise. I was saying I think this is one of those places you can only get into if you know it's a secret."

"Like an underground concert? Which in this case would be literal and figurative."

"Like a speakeasy," Lily said. "I heard those are making a comeback."

"I'm fairly sure alcohol would have to be illegal again for that kinda comeback." His voice was muted by the damp stone walls and the dark-purple lighting added to the rising creep factor.

"Okay, I think this is the bottom." She slid her foot a little farther across the level area she'd reached to be sure it was a landing. "Yep. There's a wall here too. That's nice. I thought I was starting to see things in purple. So where's the door—oh." The wall on her left wasn't a wall but a wooden door with a large iron ring bolted where the door-knob should have been. "Hey, have you ever been to a place where the door looks like it should open one way but that would be literally impossible?"

"What do you mean?"

"There's an iron ring on this side but not enough room to pull the door open."

Romeo clicked his tongue. "You're the puzzle master."

"I'm still the puzzle master's apprentice, I think. Yeah, this feels like the kinda place my mom would've loved."

"Huh." He stopped behind her—so close behind her that Lily felt his body heat radiating against her back. "I never pegged Greta as the dark, dank, and creepy type."

"No..." She slid her hands across the wooden surface, searching in the purple darkness for some kind of hidden latch or lever to open it. "It feels like a puzzle, though."

"Did you try pushing on the door?" he asked.

"Come on. If they're trying to keep this place relatively secret, they wouldn't make it that easy—"

He stretched over her shoulder to press his hand against the door. It swung away from them into another hallway from which a gold-hued light spilled into the stair-well landing.

Lily tilted her head in mild irritation. "Or these people are really into misleading handles."

"It's a good thing you have a sidekick."

"You are definitely playing the role. Well done, side-kick." She studied the short, slightly less dark hallway on the other side and slipped through the door. He followed, and as soon as he released it, the door swung back into place with nothing but a whisper against the stone floor. The silence was replaced by the sounds of animated conversation, drinks being shaken at the bar, and forks clinking against dinnerplates.

The hallway opened on the right into a long, narrow restaurant quite literally under its neighbors. Across from them, a dark, backlit wooden bar stretched along the far wall, which was only far enough away to fit four men Romeo's size standing shoulder to shoulder. The lights hanging over the bar looked like polished, upside-down tin coffee cans with bubble-shaped cutouts. Above the mirror behind the liquor shelf was a purple neon sign spelling out Le Chapeau Magique in the same swirling font as on the business card.

"It looks like we found it." Lily turned to grin at Romeo. "How do you feel about a quick detour for dinner before we start looking under rugs?"

"That would be ideal," he muttered and leaned over her shoulder to peer down the long hallway of the restaurant that stretched farther on their right. "Does that look like a tiny stage in the back to you?"

"Oh, yeah. I bet you have to be good to get a gig in here."

"Not too good," he said. "You know, if the place is supposed to be a secret."

She sent him a quick look. "Now you're catchin' on. Come on."

"Exactly like home too." He followed closely behind her. "It doesn't matter what day of the week. If there's a good bar, it's full. Do you think Montreal has a Thirst Thursdays happy hour?"

"Probably. Hey, two empty seats right there." The

high-backed bar chairs waited for them halfway down the bar. Romeo pulled her chair out first and waited for her to climb onto it. "Thank you. You know, seven years ago, you would've pulled me out of the chair instead."

"Hey, there are pros to growing up." He sat beside her, and the single bartender handling all these patrons on his own nodded at them. The man's hair was slicked back under a charcoal-gray newsboy cap, and the rest of his period ensemble was completed by a white collared shirt and a purple necktie tucked into a tailored slate-gray vest.

"He's really working the atmosphere." She leaned toward her companion and said under breath, "I bet he shined his shoes before coming into work."

"Everybody knows it's not authentic without the shoes, right?"

In less than a minute, the bartender stood in front of them across the bar and slipped two long, thin, one-page menus under their noses. "Thank you," Lily said with a smile and glanced at Romeo. His eyes were wide and his gaze was glued to the menu.

"All the drinks are on one side," the bartender explained. "Dinner options on the other. Take a look, and I'll be back when you're ready."

"Excellent."

The man had already turned away to help someone else.

"This is insane," Romeo muttered.

There were so many things he could've been referring to that Lily had to ask, "What part?"

"Seventeen dollars for a cocktail?"

"You haven't been to any of the really nice places back home, have you?"

He shot her a sideways glance. "I never saw the point."

"Then it's my treat."

"Wait, are you sure—"

"Don't." She put her menu down and pointed at him. "Don't think about money. Don't worry about who's paying. Don't even think about trying to argue. You can pick up the bill when we go on a real date." He froze for a moment in obvious surprise. "Wow. Yes, I realize I said date. And by that I meant when we go out to dinner together without...you know." She glanced around the narrow restaurant. "Ulterior motives."

"I'm not sure dinner dates don't have ulterior motives."

"You're probably right." Lily picked her menu up and pretended to read the huge list on whatever side faced her.

Romeo had returned to staring at his menu too, although when she snuck another glance at him, he was smirking. "I guess I have a date to plan."

"Only if you want to." She bit her lip and tried to wipe the smile away. The menu didn't have the name of the restaurant or any identifying information anywhere, and she couldn't focus on reading all the items. Instead, she chose the first drink on the cocktail list that made her mouth water and went with that.

Their bartender right out of *Peaky Blinders* approached them again and nodded. "What'll it be?"

"I'll have The Golden Egg, please," Lily said.

"The Expat," Romeo added.

The man looked them each in the eye as if to memorize

their faces to pair with the way they selected their drinks and nodded before he left them for the precision and alchemy of finely crafted drinks.

"You saw that drink actually has an egg in it, right?" Romeo muttered.

"Egg whites," she corrected. "It's like adding milk foam, only better."

He raised his eyebrows. "Huh. You learn something new every day."

"I think I'll add that to the list of why I like having you with me."

He laughed but kept his focus on the menu. "You're making a list?"

"It's a long one." She nodded.

"What about the cons?"

"You know, I've been so busy thinking about the pros, I haven't had a chance to sit down and write out the other half of that list. If there is one." She perused the dinner menu now, and the words looked like a different language altogether.

"Well, I can't help you with that one. No cons for me."

Lily regarded him skeptically. "Not even one?"

"Well, maybe that you went through my clothes last night—"

"Hey, I told you I didn't go through your clothes. I picked your shirt up and put it on the couch—"

"I knew it." He grinned at the menu.

"Wait—"

His laughter cut her protest short.

"Okay. I admit, I've been arguing semantics."

"Agreed. You get points for throwing me off, though. I wouldn't have noticed if I hadn't caught your scent."

"The nose never lies, huh?"

"Exactly."

"So, what looks good to you?"

His head tilted his head from side to side in indecision. "I don't know what half this stuff is."

"So let's go with the tasting menu."

"Lily, that's way too—" He stopped when she raised a finger to remind him of her previous statement. "Way too... brilliant an idea to say no."

"Nice recovery."

"See? I'm learning."

"Yeah, I think we both are."

They each ordered the dinner tasting menu made of three smaller opening courses, a palate-cleansing sorbet, an entrée, a selection of deserts, and a cup of coffee at the end. Adding drinks and a tip would bring their bill to somewhere around three hundred dollars. A little over two months before, Lily wouldn't have thought twice about it. Tonight, for the first time since her mom disappeared and the fake will took everything else, she didn't think twice about it either.

Their bartender listened attentively while they ordered and didn't once pull out a pen and notepad. She went with the summer salad, the homemade smoked salmon with truffle oil, escargot paired with lightly roasted vegetables, and the maple-glazed quail. The meal felt so much like home—like freedom and careless enjoyment without the weight of responsibilities—that she didn't pay attention to what Romeo was served for each mini course, only that he'd selected the meatiest option for everything.

"Hey, do you want to try any of mine?" She leaned back and offered him full access to her plate.

"Nope." He swallowed and looked at her. "It looks good but this is exactly what I wanted. I'm gonna stick with it."

"Well, then, more for me."

That changed when the multitude of tiny desserts arrived, all plated together and no larger than two bites each.

"Okay. I'm not a fan of tiramisu. Do you want mine?"

"I thought you'd never ask." Lily grinned and let him set the tiny desert on her plate. He eyed her citrus torte. "Yes. Please. Take it."

"Perfect." His eyes lit up before he put the whole thing in his mouth. "This is the fanciest dinner I've ever had. And I mean that in a good way."

She smiled. "Good."

"What's wrong?" He chewed slowly, swallowed, and put his fork down and turned to face her in the chair. "Hey. You look like you swallowed a bug."

"No bugs."

"What's going on?"

She took a deep breath. "This is probably gonna come out sounding self-absorbed or entitled or something."

"You aren't either of those things, Lil." The nickname made her smile. "Go ahead. Spit it out. Wait, I mean figuratively."

"It's just...I dunno. This used to be what my casual night out looked like."

"Casual, huh?" He swallowed and washed the desert down with coffee. "Well, I don't think I could do this all the time."

"Yeah, I remember saying the same thing. It's easier to get used to than you think, though."

"I bet. Do you miss it?"

Lily raised one shoulder. "Is it totally stuck-up to say yes, I miss it just a little?"

"Absolutely not. Granted, I never got whisked away by my parent into the world of fame and fortune and everything that goes with it."

She snorted. "Don't say it like that. It sounds like a Queen song."

"It is." Romeo chuckled into his coffee. "No, but seriously. It doesn't make you a bad person to miss the kinda life you were forced out of. Or into. We'd probably be sitting here, doing the same thing, even if they didn't take away everything you had." He thought for a moment, his head tilted a little. "Okay, maybe not in the Winnie."

"Yeah, I think I actually prefer the current setup. It's definitely better than flying."

"You don't like planes?"

Lily scrunched her nose. "We don't have to talk about that."

SIXTEEN

Most of the other customers at the bar seemed to enjoy their meals as much as Lily and Romeo had. One woman in a short, well-tailored gold dress sat at the bar alone, nursing something in a martini glass. A few seconds later, she was joined by a man in a sharp evening suit with a gold chain looped from a front button to his waistcoat pocket. He'd entered the underground restaurant and moved directly toward the woman in the gold dress. Her face lit up when she saw him and she tossed the neat waves of her glistening auburn hair over her shoulder before she raised a manicured hand to the man's cheek for a long, passionate kiss.

Lily looked away hastily. "Wow. Lovers reuniting at three o'clock." She nodded to their right, and Romeo snuck a quick glance.

"That's...a lot of tongue."

Snorting, she propped her elbow on the bar and leaned toward it to tuck her hair behind her ear. "Do you see anything remotely related to...you know. Business cards and broken metal trinkets?"

He frowned at her. "Hold on. I'm still trying to get that image out of my head." He looked around the restaurant again and hunched over his coffee. "There's no sign of magical clues, mysterious or otherwise."

The passionate couple stepped away from the bar.

Romeo wiped the crumbs and dessert sauces up with his finger, which he then stuck in his mouth. "Admittedly, I'm still a little distracted."

"Are you gonna lick the plate, too?" Lily grinned at him.

He whipped his head toward her and put a hand over his heart in mock insult. "I would never."

"But you were thinking about it."

Pressing his lips together, Romeo shifted his gaze evasively a few times. "Okay, you got me."

"Funny." She unslung her purse from where it hung over the back of her chair and rummaged inside for the broken piece of metal with L-A-N-T stamped along the side. Before her fingers could find it, a gaudy, high-pitched laugh came from her left. The woman in the gold dress batted her lashes furiously at the man who'd joined her at the bar. "Personally, I've never flirted that intensely in front of the bathroom." She looked at Romeo, who stared at his empty diner plate. "Okay, I'm trying to find that piece of—"

"Wait." He froze for a moment before he reached his arm out across the bar toward her. His hand hovered as he took a few quick, deep sniffs and frowned.

"What?" He eyed her briefly like an afterthought and sniffed again. His frown deepened. "Romeo, what's going on?" Lily took a few of her own experimental whiffs. "I only smell coffee, but I know that doesn't really mean anything. But you look really confused."

"What?" His attention returned fully to her. "No. It's... well, it's gone now." He turned halfway in his chair to search the narrow restaurant. "It's not like anybody could hide it in a place as cramped as this, but..." His nose scrunched like he was about to sneeze.

"Hide what?"

His eyes shifted around the restaurant one more time before he leaned toward her. "Magic."

"Oh. That's actually a really good lead I honestly did not expect right now."

"Right? Most of the time, it's merely a spark in the air, then it's gone."

She narrowed her eyes and took another glance at the restaurant. "And right now doesn't fall into the 'most of the time' category, does it?"

"No." Somehow, the purple neon lighting of the Le Chapeau Magique sign behind the bar made the gold flecks in his green eyes look like tiny flames. "Just now...it was definitely the same smell. But like ten times stronger."

"Well, if it was really strong magic..." Lily took a long sip of ice water.

"Not the strength of it, Lily. The amount."

"How much?"

"A lot. All in one place." Romeo sniffed the air again but shook his head. "Then it simply disappeared, and I don't know how—" He shifted the other way in his chair to glance toward the stage on the far-right wall and the three full, recessed booths behind them.

"Okay." She patted his forearm that had settled on the bar, and he whirled to face her. "If there's considerable magic here, we should be careful looking for it. Subtle, right?"

"Sorry." He blinked and leaned back in his chair again. "It totally threw me for a minute."

She removed her hand and pulled her wallet out. "That's totally okay. We'll figure this out." She placed her one credit card on the bar and assumed their astute bartender would get the hint as she nodded at Romeo. "Do you think you'd know it if you smelled it again? The same amount?"

"About as well as you'd know a werewolf shifting right in front of you." His gaze darted across the room again and behind her toward the short hall at the entrance.

"Yeah, that's fairly obvious. Well, let me know if it happens again."

"Oh, you'll know."

The bartender returned swiftly and didn't even ask if they were ready for the check before he nodded slightly at Lily and discretely collected her card.

A muffled conversation rose behind them. Two gentlemen—they were entirely dressed like gentlemen— emerged from the entrance hallway and headed toward the bar.

"And you caught him doing it?" the first man asked and dug at his teeth with a toothpick.

Is that a cravat? Lily darted repeated glances at the duo.

"I caught him with the book open and the damn mirror right next to it on the table," the second man said. He jerked a finger toward the floor for emphasis and shook his head. "The balls on that one. I'm tellin' ya."

"That's why I make all my prospects run the gauntlet first," Mr. Cravat said as they reached the bar two seats down on the other side of Romeo. "All the apprentices think they're hot shit. If you make them prove themselves first, it's like taking your pick of the finest geldings. It guarantees that they know their place."

The bartender approached the newcomers without a word, two drinks already in hand. Mr. Cravat and his friend with the apprentice problem—who wore a dinner jacket with a black satin lapel—nodded curtly and lifted their drinks from the bar without sitting down. "Sure," Dinner Jacket said. "That works until they've learned enough from you to step out on their own. Then guess what their first order of business is gonna be?"

"Don't remind me." Mr. Cravat glanced at the ceiling as both men drained their drinks in one swallow. Two empty glasses clunked onto the bar again before the men headed toward Lily, past her and the restaurant's entrance, and to the opposite end of the room.

"That Matthews boy gave you one helluva run for your money," Dinner Jacket added.

"What part of 'don't remind me' did you not get?" Mr. Cravat brushed the sleeves of his jacket off. "I came here to enjoy myself, Wilson."

Two seconds later, Mr. Cravat looked at Lily and his gaze triggered a confusing jolt of something she couldn't name rippling through her. She looked quickly toward the short entrance hall and pretended to be waiting for someone else to join her at the bar. "Did you hear that?"

"What?" Romeo sniffed the air again, a confused expression on his face, and took sip of coffee.

"Those two guys."

"Nope. Sorry. I'm focusing on the...smells."

"Fair enough. Romeo, they were talking about mirrors and books and apprentices. Honestly, I think they were witches. Or some kind of magical. It's not all that weird with the Order of North's sigil on the front door. But nobody else here has done anything remotely...well, magical. That wouldn't be a totally weird conversation to overhear if I wasn't already listening for it. But if those men were—"

"Magic," he whispered.

"Well, yeah. Of some kind or another."

"No, I mean it's..." He clenched his eyes shut, then jerked them open. "Man, that's intense."

She turned toward the end of the restaurant and the restrooms. "It might have something to do with—wait a minute."

"What?"

"Did they go into the bathroom?" Mr. Cravat and Dinner Jacket were gone.

Romeo tipped his head back, sniffed again, and uttered a low growl. "I lost it again. What the hell can keep that much magic from seeping out all the time?"

"More magic, if I had to guess." Lily leaned back in her chair and studied the end of the hallway. "The woman in the gold dress never came out of the bathroom. Neither did her date. I think I know where it's coming from. Hang out here for a minute. Hey, don't look so disappointed. We're close. I promise." She slipped off the high bar chair and slung her purse over her shoulder.

"Where are you going?" Romeo stared at her, his expression wary.

"I have to go...powder my nose." Her shoulder raised in a playful shrug.

"No, you don't."

"Correct." She grinned. "But I need you to roll with it." Before he could protest, she turned and hurried to the restrooms, walking quickly enough to make the urgency of excusing herself perfectly believable. This side of the establishment was painted an almost blue-black, with the same design of purple bubbles as was on the business card. There were only three doors—Men's, Ladies', and Emergency Exit with a sign warning everyone of the promised alarm should some smartass try to slip out the back. The crash bar on that door was very real. "Yeah, I would've heard that opening and closing if Ms. Gold Dress, her date, and those two gentlemen went out that way. It's definitely not the best choice for entering a hidden room if non-magicals think it was a real emergency exit." She eyed the Ladies' room door. "Maybe it is the bathrooms, then," she muttered. "Because I know there's some kind of door here." Without breaking her stride, she pushed the door to the women's restroom open and slipped inside.

It was empty. She peeped into all three stalls, looked behind the main door, and checked either side of the sink in case. There was no broom closet, no trap door, and nothing that moved or blinked or made a sound. "Yeah, I bet there's no magical scent in here, either." She stepped up to the sink and studied herself in the mirror. "Okay." She huffed out a sigh. "Forget the fact that I'm reasonably sure we're both severely underdressed. If I ran a joint like this, where would I put it?" Leaning forward to swipe a stray eyelash off her cheek, she paused. "Right out in the open where everyone can see it. Only not everyone would. Because who's gonna look for it unless they know it's there? Yeah. That's a good start." She straightened her lace blouse, fluffed the ruffled quarter-length sleeves on her shoulders, and turned to open the restroom door.

"Oh...this is what I missed the first time." The men's restroom was directly opposite the women's, but to the left of the men's room door at about chest height, one of the lavender bubbles had been painted with a darker symbol inside it. "There you are, you sneaky Order of North sigil." With a satisfied smirk, she returned to the bar. Once she'd clambered onto the seat again, she met Romeo's confused gaze and wiggled her eyebrows.

"It looks like you found something," he said.

She grinned. "I did. And you are coming with me to check it out." The credit card receipt and a pen had been left with the return of her card, so she quickly added a twenty-five-percent tip and slipped the card back into her wallet. "If I'm wrong, I guess we'll look like a couple of tourists without a clue what they're getting into and we'll have to find another way."

"But you don't think you're wrong, do you?" He narrowed his eyes and chewed the inside of his cheek.

"Not even a little. Follow my lead, and you'll be fine." She nodded at him and hoped he got the picture through her pleasant smile. After a moment, she slipped off the chair again and waited for him to do the same. He drained the rest of his coffee, and she linked her arm through his to tug him gently toward the restrooms. "I said you wouldn't regret dinner first." She raised her voice a hair above speaking volume.

He frowned at her. "What are you talking about?"

"This is all for show," she said through almost gritted teeth. "Roll with it." She raised her voice again. "You're impossible. It is okay to admit you're wrong every once in a while." Her raised eyebrow was her attempt to remind him subtly of the act.

After a momentary hesitation, he shoved his free hand into the pocket of his shorts and stopped with her at the end of the hall. "Well, if tonight goes the way I hope it does, you might convince me to agree with you."

"Good work," she muttered.

When he turned halfway toward her and put his back to the restaurant, it provided the perfect opportunity for him to hide his confusion—and for Lily to still have the view she wanted of the bartender. "It's a wall," he whispered.

She looked at him, stepped closer, and put her hand on his chest. "Pretend you're saying something really sweet to me." His brows drew together but he raised his hand gently to brush her hair away from her eyes and tuck it behind her ear. "Yeah." Her eyelashes fluttered. "Like that."

The minute she glanced past him at the bar, Romeo said, "I don't have to pretend something like that."

"Wait for it..." The bartender set two drinks in front of two other patrons, looked up, and met Lily's gaze. He gave her a small, almost imperceptible nod before he turned away and seamlessly turned his attention to his customers.

"Lily," Romeo said, "I probably should've told you this—"

"Yes. I was right." The words slipped out of her before she could stop them, but her finger was already on its way toward the lavender bubble on the wall with the Order of North's sigil painted inside it. "He nodded at me, Romeo. Now's our opening." The bubble retracted into the wall with a barely audible click before the entire section of wall between the men's restroom and the emergency exit popped open by half an inch. "Not only a wall," she said as she pushed the hidden door open and pulled him along behind her. "It's also a secret entrance."

SEVENTEEN

The door closed behind them on its own when they stepped completely through. "Okay, first, I want to be perfectly clear that I didn't try to blow you off—woah." What they found on the other side of Le Chapeau Magique's hidden entrance wiped everything else from her mind. "Okay, I've been to parties with magicals. But this... this is for magicals."

They had stepped into a massive circular room with a horseshoe bar in the middle. The same purple lanterns that had lit the stairwell from Crescent Street now illuminated the entire space, except these levitated in the air and floated at random so the light shifted and changed every second. Tiny beads that looked like pearls swirled immediately below the dark, painted ceiling, which made the area look much bigger than it was.

Above the constant buzz of so many simultaneous conversations, a woman's low, husky voice sang a little jazz number in French. Another woman shrieked in enjoyment and laughed. The woman in the gold dress clapped in delight as a magical somewhere conjured a live white rabbit from a hat that floated in midair, made of nothing but golden sparkles. Orange smoke billowed from the other side of the bar but didn't seem to make it past the counter. Three bartenders worked behind the horseshoe, all of them in purple sequined vests over black shirts. They mixed patrons' drinks not by pouring liquor but by summoning it out of the bottles. The alcohol arced through the air into shakers like a glittering, multi-colored water fountain. All along the perimeter of the circular room were arched doorways, spaced five or six feet apart. "Those doors are spinning," Lily muttered. "Or maybe it's the walls?" Each door was lit with a soft light in a different color.

"Do you see this?" she asked Romeo, unable to take her eyes off the illusory spells and the flashy costumes. "It's a freakin' magical speakeasy." He grunted behind her and this was followed by a tug before his arm slipped out of hers. He thumped against the wall like someone had actually struck him. "Woah, there." He squeezed his eyes shut tightly and shook his head. "Are you okay?"

He grunted again, and his now open eyes rolled for a second before his gaze settled on her face. "Woah."

"I'm gonna take that as a yes." Lily laughed and grabbed his arm again to help him off the wall. "Because I know you've seen magic before."

"This is definitely what I smelled." He swayed a little until she put a hand on his chest to steady him. "Being in it is like... It's like waking up still drunk."

"Well, admittedly, I can relate to that. Do you think you can pull it together and handle yourself in here?"

Romeo glanced across the room, focused on her again, and took a deep breath. "I dunno."

"Well, try because I really need you to be on alert right now. Running at full capacity, Romeo. Can you do that too?"

"Maybe if I knew how."

"Okay. Well..." She straightened his shirt, readjusted his lopsided collar, and patted his chest. "Try to breathe through your mouth, then. I know we're not really dressed for this 1920s costume party in July, but do your best to fit in, huh?" With her arm linked through his again, she stepped into the room to continue her exploration but kept a tight grip on him with both hands. "Hey, if you feel dizzy again, let me know. We'll find a way to not draw more attention to ourselves than we have to."

"Sure."

Most of the people in there were witches. Almost all were dressed for a period of at least a hundred years before, although she noticed three women huddled together at the bar who wore pastel-colored shorts and spaghetti-strap tank tops. "They're not much older than me."

"Who?"

"Those girls at the bar. I'm willing to bet this is their first fancy party in a secret, underground speakeasy frequented only by magicals. Maybe even their first bar, period. Wait—woah. That's a warlock."

"For real?"

Lily shrugged and stared at the being with long,

straight black hair swept back from a high forehead who wore a black, robe-like costume. "Okay, I'm mostly sure. I've never seen one in person, but I've read more than enough about them to—oh. Yeah. That's a warlock." She glanced at Romeo and pointed to her face with two fingers before whispering, "Red eyes."

He seemed to have found his legs again in the sea of witches entertaining themselves. "You know, it made sense why the restaurant would be Le Chapeau Magique," he said. "Until I saw this place right here. This is the real Magic Hat, isn't it?"

"Yeah, I'd have to agree with you on that one."

They wandered around, taking in the glittering baubles and the Blackjack table that dealt itself and the empty glasses that removed themselves from surfaces simply by vanishing altogether. Three creatures the size of tennis balls scurried across the black-and-white checkered tiles and across Lily's shoe—a cross between a mouse and a frog but covered in soot-gray feathers. She leaned into Romeo and turned to watch them scamper away between all the expensive shoes on every witch's feet. No one else noticed the creatures, who somehow avoided being stepped on.

"I think my arm's gonna fall asleep," he said in her ear.

"Oh. Sorry." Lily loosened her grasp and looked at him. "Did you see those little...things?"

He offered her a half-smile. "Nope. Take a look at that, though."

A small stage stood on the far side of the room. The

jazz singer's smoky voice raised again for a new song, this time in a duet, but only one woman stood on the stage in front of the microphone. The duet part came from the huge snake head that sang into the microphone beside her —and the fact that the head grew from the dip between the woman's neck and her shoulder like an extra limb. "Is it weird to say that I still like the music?" Lily asked.

Romeo snorted. "Not any weirder than anything else here."

"You sound like you have a cold."

"I'm trying not to breathe through my nose. Like you said."

"Is it helping?"

He raised his eyebrows. "Yeah, actually."

"Ladies and gentlemen." A loud, eccentric male voice came from nowhere and everywhere. "In two minutes, we reach the top of the hour again. All hourglasses will be reset and all rooms emptied. Ask our masters of mixology at the bar for available openings behind every door. It's all first come, first serve, so don't let your fantasies slip through your fingers."

"I think I already know the answer," Romeo said and studied the rising activity after the announcement. "But I still have to ask. Not all magic-related things are as weird as this, right?"

"Not the kind I know. But my mom definitely wouldn't have brought me to a place like this anyway."

"Okay. That's still reassuring."

Lily glanced casually around the room again. "But she

did send me here for a reason. I don't think it was to get in on all the fantasies behind those rotating doors." Most of the patrons now moved toward the horseshoe bar, vying to be the first to get served the object of their requests. "Hey, maybe that business card is actually like a calling card. Or a coupon."

"Wait, did it say coupon anywhere?" He couldn't wrap his head around her point as she dragged him behind her.

"Well, no. But I'm following another hunch. Come on."

"Lily, this isn't exactly how I imagined finding out what your fantasies are."

She grinned at him. "But you did imagine them, then?"

He smiled, opened his mouth, and took a breath to say something. They were jostled by a short, overweight bald man who dragged a rail-thin woman with a fringed silver dress behind him toward the bar.

"We'll come back to that." She released his arm so she could take his hand and towed him to the bar in very much the same way. His surprised laughter rang out behind her.

This was most likely like placing illegal bets on horseraces in the early 1900s. The witches crowded around the bar and shouted out different colors and numbers to the bartenders. A few waved random slips of paper above their heads, and the servers took the whole thing in stride. They made eye contact with specific witches, nodded at some, shook their heads at others, pointed in various directions, accepted some of the papers fluttering their way, and moved on to the next one in seconds.

The woman with the snake growing out of her neck struck a massive gong at the back of the speakeasy, and the commotion instantly died. A few magicals remained at the bar, laughing and ordering drinks. Some shook their heads and walked away looking entirely dejected. Those who'd gotten what they wanted from the two minutes of chaos hurried toward the perimeter of the room, where they stared at the rotating wall of doors and waited for their chosen room to find them.

Finally, one of the bartenders was free long enough to approach Lily. His red beard was sprinkled with purple glitter, and he nodded at her first, then Romeo. "What's your pleasure?" He snapped his fingers and pointed straight up into the air. A column of bright-pink, bubbling liquid rose from the liquor shelves behind him and dove over his head into the shaker he'd set on the bar.

"Hi." She smiled and batted her eyelashes. "Is the owner in tonight?"

Purple Beard snapped again. The deliciously overpowering fumes of bourbon filled the air before a few shots of it streaked over his shoulder and into the silver shaker. "He stepped out a few hours ago but should be back fairly soon."

"Okay. Is there somewhere I can wait for him?" It was almost impossible to focus on talking when he snapped with both hands, clapped, and twirled his fingers in front of his chest. A few drops of bitters fell into the shaker from out of nowhere before he put the lid on to shake it vigorously.

He poured the contents into a rocks glass in three seconds before an orange peel rose on its own from behind the bar and zested itself onto the surface of the drink, which then promptly lit up with purple flame. The rocks glass and its cocktail contents slid down the bar, turned perfectly at the bend in the horseshoe, and stopped in front of its owner. "Do you have an appointment?"

"Well, I have this...hold on." She rummaged through her purse, conscious of the fact that both Purple Beard and Romeo had settled curious gazes on her. Finally, she pulled out the business card for Le Chapeau Magique and handed it toward the bartender.

He raised an eyebrow, looked at Romeo, and stared at the card. His hand jerked out with impossible speed to snatch the card from her fingers before he pocketed it quickly and set to work making someone else's order without ever touching a bottle of booze. "Black door. You can wait inside." Purple Beard studied Romeo again. He narrowed his eyes while two streams of what looked like champagne arced over his shoulders, crossed in front of his chest, and rose in a twisting spiral before they fell into a gold-colored shaker.

"Right," Lily said. "Thank you." She grabbed her companion's hand and whisked him away from the bar.

"I think he knows," Romeo said, looking briefly over his shoulder.

"Knows what?"

"What I am."

They skirted around a woman in a silver-sequined vest balancing a stack of at least a dozen full, bubbling champagne flutes on the top of her head. "Wow. How does she serve those? Never mind. Even if he knows, Romeo, he didn't say anything about it. And he didn't stop us. So I'm fairly sure you're still on the list of acceptable customers. And I got us one step closer to whatever my mom wanted me to find here. As long as that's what the business card was for 'cause I don't think I'll be getting that back."

"Unless it's a trap," he muttered.

She clicked her tongue at him. "If they didn't want you in here, I don't think they would've let you in. Magical security being what it is." They pushed their way through the crowd toward the outer wall, which still spun clockwise but had slowed. To her left stood a woman in a bright-turquoise evening gown and peacock feathers protruded from the intricate, braided bun on the top of her head. A white ferret nestled in the crook of her arm as she stroked its fur eagerly in a rhythmic motion while she waited.

"Oh, look." Romeo nodded at the ferret. "It likes you."

Lily cleared her throat. "I think it's simply staring at me. That doesn't look like adoration." On her right were the overweight bald man and the incredibly thin woman, who pinched his cheeks and pursed her lips at him in some kind of lovers' baby talk while he giggled.

The two friends stood in front of the black circle painted on a white tile about a foot away from the rotating wall. Both parties on either side of her stood behind their own circles also painted on white tiles—the woman and her ferret had picked maroon, while the sickeningly affectionate, oddly paired couple waited in front of the pea-green one. "Black circle. Black door. Okay, I guess this is where we need to be." Lily stepped closer to the circle and took a deep breath. She couldn't help but take another quick glance at the ferret in the woman's arms. "Yeah, that thing's totally staring at me." The animal uttered a surprisingly loud squeak, she jumped, and she realized the peacock-feathered woman had been staring at her too.

"Oh, I know, Archibald," the woman cooed as she stroked the ferret and scrutinized Lily with a raised eyebrow. "What's that?" She glanced at her furry white pet and shook her head. "Hush up. That's her business."

Romeo bent to whisper in her ear. "That sounds like taking the whole witch's familiar thing to a whole new level."

Lily blinked and turned to the wall, where the doors moved slowly enough now that she caught a glimpse through each passing window—a large, empty swimming pool, a red couch half-hidden by silk drapes, an elephant...

"Please tell me you saw the elephant," she said with a hasty glance at Romeo.

He stood beside her, still holding her hand, and chewed on the inside of his cheek. "Yeah, that's what it looked like. So be ready to throw some of those red sparks, okay? Just in case."

His grasp was almost uncomfortably tight, but she ignored it. The wall came to a complete stop and each door glowed with the same color as the circle painted on the floor in front of it. Except for theirs. The black door was exactly that—completely black—and it didn't have a window.

All around the perimeter of the room, the witches

who'd snagged themselves an hour in the weird room of their choice stepped forward, and each door opened in response. Lily took a deep breath. "Here's to hoping this is exactly where Mom wanted us to be right now." Together, they stepped forward to find out for themselves what the rest of Le Chapeau Magique never got to see.

EIGHTEEN

The room was incredibly dark when they entered and, of course, the door closed behind them. Romeo glared at it, and Lily put a hand on her hip. "Well, this is a little disappointing."

The apparently infamous black door within Le Chapeau Magique was nothing more than an office. A long bookshelf stretched across the entire left wall from floor to ceiling, filled not only with books but a few contraptions that attempted to be model airplanes, what looked like an oversized Magic 8-Ball, different-colored stones of various shapes and sizes, and a taxidermized chipmunk. Two armchairs upholstered in crushed red velvet faced away from the bookshelf, with a low teak coffee table centered between them. A large wooden desk stood in front of the far wall, covered in scattered paperwork, a closed laptop, and a vase of dying tulips. On the wall itself was a massive painting of the heron silhouette, its wings spread in flight and neck bent in a u-shape, as if it had been taken from the business card. Or vice versa. "If everything about seeing the bird was really supposed to help me instead of eliminate me, I'd say this looks like the right place." Lily stepped into the room for a closer inspection of the bookshelf.

"But it still doesn't feel...right, does it?"

"No. It sure doesn't."

"So now we're looking for the rest of that metal piece?" Romeo stooped to stick his nose almost directly onto the stuffed chipmunk, which had been suspended forever in a position of eagerly anticipating the seed it clutched between tiny paws.

She went to the desk and peered at the scattered paperwork. Most of it was itemized billing for restaurant and entertainment expenses. One page looked like a fan letter, which she stopped reading when she got to: *I have to confess, I've imagined you in the silver room with me for the last three weeks.* "This place is so weird. I'm not sure how we're supposed to find a chunk of metal in all this. Honestly, I would've thrown it away if I found it and didn't know it meant something. We don't even know that the other half's here."

Romeo turned away from the bookshelf to look at her. "If you actually believed that, we wouldn't have made it this far." She shrugged, tapped one of the dying tulips, and drew her hand back when a crispy petal broke away and fluttered to the desk's surface. "Isn't there some kind of tracking spell you can use?"

She raised an eyebrow. "To track a piece of junk when it decides to get up and walk away?"

"Like a Find-My-iPhone spell or something." He

peered over the back of the armchair and frowned at the velvet cushions. "You know. Like using the part you have to...I dunno. Call the part you don't have."

"Your magical-phone metaphor is a stretch." Lily shrugged and ran her fingers along the back of the other armchair. "But actually, I think I know what you mean. That was helpful."

"Hey, that's what I'm here for." Romeo grinned and stumbled when the armchair he'd leaned on scooted forward across the floor.

"All right. Gimme a sec." She slung her purse off her shoulder, dropped it on the desk, and sifted through everything she'd put in there over the last two months. *I really need to clean this thing out.* Finally, she found the broken silver piece that could have been a wings or flames or something else with jagged edges and the raised letters 'LANT' running up the side. Twisting the piece until the broken side faced her—where she could see the dull metal beneath the shiny silver that was probably only paint—she frowned. "Here goes."

She tapped the broken end and drew a horizontal line in the air from left to right, leaving behind a thin purple shimmer. "So let's find the other piece of you, then." Taking a breath, she leaned toward the purple line of her spell and blew on it like it was a candle on a birthday cake. The thin line dispersed in every direction around the office and filtered into nothingness. Romeo smirked. "That's so much better to watch than all that circus crazy out there."

"Well, I'm glad you liked it, but I don't think it worked." Lily turned as she searched for any flash of purple light or shimmer or something to prove they were in the right place. "Huh. "So..." She frowned at the broken fragment in her hand and snatched her purse off the desk. "That spell almost always does the trick. I guess we should look somewhere—"

The desk thumped, shook, and rattled a stray pen across the papers until it dropped onto the floor. Lily jumped back and stared at it.

"What was that?" Romeo asked, suddenly at her side.

"Wow. You can be really fast when you want to, huh?"

He merely nodded at the desk. The thump came again, only this time, one of the drawers vibrated in place instead of the whole piece of furniture shaking. "Sure. I'm really fast, and you're a skilled witch. I think your spell worked."

"It's possible. Then again, you could be right about us walking into a trap. If there's anything really important here, there are bound to be some safeguards in place. Maybe wards. At the very least, an automatic alarm." With a deep breath, Lily summoned a ball of flame in her palm. It gave off a fairly bright light but also armed her with something to throw at whatever had jumped in that drawer. She glanced at Romeo, who was tense and alert and stared at the desk with a flash of bright silver in his irises. "Good. We're both ready." She stepped forward and reached slowly for the rattling desk drawer with one hand while she raised her fireball with the other.

When she'd wrapped her fingers around the knob, she jerked the drawer open and stepped back. Nothing rocketed out. Nothing leapt or crawled or oozed. In fact, nothing happened at all. Even the drawer seemed to assume that the thumps were no longer necessary. "Do you smell anything?" she asked.

"Nope."

"So nothing you smell, and nothing I can see. I'd say that's a good sign." Swallowing, she stepped toward the drawer and peered over the edge. She extinguished the fireball in an anticlimactic little puff of air because she definitely didn't need it. "It's a junk drawer."

"Huh?" He joined her behind the desk and looked into the open drawer with her—receipts, candy wrappers, over a dozen pens, a couple of purple marbles, and a set of keys half-buried under all of it. "Wait a minute." He fumbled for the keys and lifted them with a little jingle. "Do you still think your spell didn't work?"

Lily gaped at him, then at the keys, and laughed. "You have a really good eye." She took them from him and studied the three different charms hanging from the ring. One was merely a black diamond, which was essentially boring. The second was a two-inch top hat covered in purple glitter. The last charm was two-thirds of some kind of silver leaf, and the other third had been broken off.

She cast a quick look at Romeo and wiggled her eyebrows. "Not wings and not fire. It's a maple leaf."

"Hey, at least I took a few guesses." He smirked.

Lily lined up the two pieces of the keyring charm—which apparently belonged to the owner of Le Chapeau Magique, whoever he was—until they fit perfectly into place along the broken seam. "Yep. This is definitely the—ow!" A bright flash of purple filled the seam between the pieces, and the metal leaf zapped her fingers with warm energy.

"Are you okay?" Romeo asked.

"Yeah, it...it didn't actually hurt. It was more like getting shocked with static. And apparently, we used my mom's clue to make another clue." Now the letters 'LANT' along the side of Lily's broken piece made much more sense. The recently restored keychain charm now read 'Mont Tremblant National Park' in capital letters. "Have you ever heard of this place?"

"No, but I can—crap. No cell service. Is that a magic thing too?"

She shook. "I'm reasonably sure it's simply an under-ground thing."

"Right."

"So these—oh." She'd tried to pull the pieces apart again, but they were now completely reattached. "You know, I really can't tell if my Mom set all this up or if this thing was already magical before she broke a piece off for herself. Either way, I guess I fixed the charm."

"Really?" Romeo peered at the item in her hand and shrugged. "At least we know where we're going now. So put the keys back and we'll get outta here."

"What?" Lily pulled the keys toward her chest before she realized what she was doing and lowered her hands. "No. My mom left me that piece and I'm not leaving it here."

"Lily..." He pointed at the drawer.

"She wanted me to have the whole thing, Romeo. I know it. So I'm keeping it." She raised her eyebrow and promptly dropped the maple-leaf charm and the keys into her purse.

"You're gonna get us in trouble."

"Only if we get caught." She adjusted the strap of her purse over her shoulder and tapped the center of his chest. "And we make an excellent team. Let's get outta here."

Shaking his head, Romeo followed her back toward the office door and Lily turned the doorknob to step out into the circular room of Le Chapeau Magique's backroom circus party for witches.

"Woah." She braced herself against the doorway, assaulted by spinning visual tracers of orange smoke, flashing baubles, sparkling purple lanterns, and all the magical people gathered in various shades of early-twentieth-century costuming. "When did these rooms start spinning again?"

"I have no idea. I didn't feel anything." Romeo's hand thumped against the doorframe above hers. "But this is definitely making me dizzy."

"It had to have started when we stepped into this room to be going at this speed again, right?"

"Maybe it's that big room with the bar that's actually spinning."

"We would've stepped onto a moving floor when we left the restaurant." Lily looked across the room—where no one seemed to notice two underdressed magicals peering out of an open black door—and found the extremely normal-looking door through which they'd entered. As each colored door spun toward the entrance, it disappeared behind the regular door before reappearing on the other side with the rotation like all the moving doors were nothing more than lights from a spinning projector in the center of the club. Except they were real because people had walked through them. She and Romeo had stepped through this one too. "We need to get off this magical merry-go-round."

"Yep."

They were approaching the entrance door again and were about to pass the back of the horseshoe bar. She grabbed his hand, and on the count of three, they stepped through the spinning door that didn't physically feel like it was spinning at all. "That was easy—"

A shrieking alarm like a high-school period bell sounded in short, two-second bursts. The entire club of costumed witches paused and almost every one of them turned to stare at the lone witch and her werewolf friend who'd quite clearly broken the rules. "Or not," Romeo muttered.

A man in an all-black business suit—black shirt, black tie, and black jacket—turned away from speaking with Purple Beard behind the horseshoe bar. The horrendous scowl he directed at Lily, paired with the shiny silver pin on his lapel with the Order of North's symbol, demanded her full attention. But he also drew his right arm back to throw something at her.

"Get down!" she shouted. The conversation hushed, but the ringing alarm continued to pierce through every other noise. She dipped into a crouch and pulled hard on Romeo's hand seconds before Black Suit's bolt of searing red attack spell careened over their heads and crackled against the spinning wall behind them.

"Is this really a shoot first, ask questions later kinda deal?" Romeo grunted and stumbled forward in his crouch when Lily jerked her hand out of his and straightened quickly.

She launched a stun spell at Black Suit, who stepped aside and let his master of mixology take the hit for him instead. Purple Beard uttered a yelp of surprise, went as rigid as a board, and fell back like a fallen tree. When Le Chapeau Magique's patrons realized their gracious host hadn't dealt with the issue immediately—and that issue was now fighting back—the huge circular room erupted into chaos. Women screamed and ran for cover when two giant men wearing all black and bright-purple neckties launched twin streams of electric-green energy over the crowded room. Lily ducked and flicked her wrist to send one of the magical bouncers stumbling into the other. "Okay, new plan."

Growling, Romeo straightened beside her. "You need a wolf."

"Nope. Door." She grabbed his hand again and yanked him around as the spinning door outlined in orange lights approached. Without hesitation, she pushed it open and leapt inside.

"What the—" Romeo stared directly ahead at a man in the center of this room, his arms suspended out to the sides at his shoulders while he sobbed his heart out.

"Uh...sorry to interrupt," Lily said and spun to see Black Suit stalking after them and toward the orange room.

"Head in the game, please, Romeo." Summoning blue flames at the tips of her fingers, she took careful aim and flicked all of them at once. The flames launched from her hand and immediately caught on the hem of Black Suit's pantlegs. He shouted in surprise and had to ignore her in order to fight the fire that had already begun to climb up his calves. "Yeah, good luck with that. It took me a month to learn how to put those out."

A crackling green bolt flashed through the doorway and barely missed her face when she darted to the side. Instead, it struck the man who'd apparently stepped into this room to have a meltdown. The sobbing stopped and the witch's eyes rolled back in his head, but whatever magic held him kept him suspended right there.

"Hey, there's another door," Romeo shouted.

"There are lots of doors."

"I mean a...normal door!" When he pointed, Lily peered around the doorway in the direction the spinning wall was taking them and saw the white, stationary door opposite the hidden club's entrance and behind the stage.

"Are you kidding me? That lady and her snakehead are still singing right now. Okay. Normal door. It's worth a shot. We'll get off right before it shows up. Got it?"

"Yup."

One of the club's patrons decided to try being a hero and grabbed hold of the orange doorway. Romeo growled and slammed his fist down on the man's manicured fingers. A scream was followed by a crash and the tinkle of broken glass.

"All right. Let's go." They surged out of the door

together in front of what was hopefully an emergency exit. Unfortunately, they hadn't thought to check who followed closely behind the rotating orange room. Massive hands clamped down on Lily's shoulders and jerked her back. She lost her footing and her tailbone flared with jarring pain when it made instant contact with the checkered tile floor.

One of the bouncers with a purple tie stalked past her toward Romeo, who'd spun to face the man with a snarl. The bouncer landed one good right hook to his jaw, but the werewolf bounced back with surprising speed. He glared at his attacker, who was at least three inches taller and wider at the shoulders, and growled again with another silver flash behind his irises.

Lily struggled to push herself back to her feet. Her back screamed at her, but she'd had more than enough practice brushing off the pain of being tossed around on the training mat. She paused when the bouncer who had squared off against Romeo reacted in the strangest way to seeing a werewolf in the club for witches only. The man growled back—loud and feral—and Romeo blinked in surprise. "What—"

The bouncer swept a massive fist into Romeo's gut and pounded the breath out of him.

"Hey!" Lily shouted. The giant whirled and sneered at her. She released the strongest attack spell she knew, and the red sparks that erupted from both hands rocketed into the bouncer's chest with a thump like an ax striking a tree. It catapulted him across the perimeter of the room, where he crashed into the small stage and launched the singer to tumble off the edge with a hiss from both her mouths. "Are you good?" Lily took Romeo's shoulders and helped him straighten fully again.

"Yeah." He grunted, looked up, and swept his arm around her and almost threw her against the wall.

"What—" She turned in the same moment that a flash of intensely bright yellow grazed his ribs and brought a roar of pain from his open mouth. Black Suit had learned how to put the blue fire out and he now stormed toward them. Another flash of yellow light grew in his outstretched hand. Even the light looked sharp enough to do real damage, and the man's previous scowl had morphed into a sickly, twisted grin beneath wild eyes.

When Lily clapped her hands together, she cast the only spell that came to mind. It was supposed to be an illusory wall—a screen to show her and Romeo frozen there in fear to distract Black Suit while they actually bolted toward the exit. But when she spread her hands and opened the space between them, a thick black cloud mushroomed in front of her. It grew and churned, crackled like rolling thunder, and continued to grow. Black Suit stopped dead in his tracks and in the next moment, she could no longer see him.

"Take it down!" a man shouted, followed by more shrieks and demands to contain whatever she had unleashed before it swallowed the circular room.

"What the hell is that?" She took a step back and stared at the unintentional spell she'd cast, gaping as it roiled and ballooned all the way to the ceiling and to the floor. It stretched out in every direction away from her and Romeo.

"Good work. Time to go." He grabbed her hand and yanked her away from the black cloud. Somehow, the screams on the other side of it sounded thick and muted and really far away.

She forced herself to pay attention and jogged the few feet toward what she really hoped was the exit. Romeo stumbled a few times, but they reached it and both put their weight against the door and shoved it open.

NINETEEN

Since they'd opened the first unmarked door with the purple circle on Crescent Street, each one after that led the duo to completely unexpected places. Le Chapeau Magique's emergency exit was no different. Lily stared in confusion at the wide concrete wall barely five feet away, and Romeo's shoes scuffed on the asphalt seconds before the door closed behind them. A little disoriented, she whirled and froze. Of all the things she expected to see, the only one present was Romeo. Everything else was gone—the magical club, the door, the walls, all of it. Instead of the rear of the underground speakeasy sandwiched between The Winston Churchill Pub and Thursday's, she peered down a dark, narrow alley that stretched all the way between the other establishments toward Crescent Street.

"What was that?" Romeo winced and doubled over, clutching at his side.

"I have no idea but we can figure that one out later. Are you okay?"

"Yeah." He grunted through another grimace and turned to look around them. "Uh...I have a feeling that just because we can't see the door doesn't mean no one can come after us. So maybe let's—" He blew out a deep sigh. As if to prove his point, a loud banging echoed behind the row of restaurants, seemingly from where the door would've been in the alley.

"Okay, right." Lily put his arm around her shoulder and helped him stumble down the narrow street between the cement wall on their right and the long row of attached restaurants on their left. The only light came from those turned on over the back doors of every restaurant they passed. It had to be at least after 9:00 p.m. by now and the sky was completely black. *Like that cloud...* A tiny shudder went through her.

When they reached Boulevard de Maisonneuve, Romeo slowed and leaned back against the corner of the building. A tense sigh escaped him, and now that they'd stepped into the brighter glow of the streetlamps, she saw the dark stain of blood on his shirt.

"Oh, my God." She stepped closer to him and pulled his hands away from his side. "No, no. Oh, jeeze. Are you—"

"I'm fine," he said as he slowed his heavy breathing and placed one hand against his side.

"No, you're not. You're bleeding. I've never seen a spell cut like that before." She tried to remove his hand.

"Lily, really. I'm okay."

Her lower lip trembled. "We need to get you somewhere safe. I'm so sorry. I didn't want you to get hurt. I thought... This was supposed to be..."

Romeo merely chuckled, closed his eyes, and rested his head against the brick wall behind him.

"It's really not funny. I'm gonna chalk that up to blood loss. Let me see," she whispered.

"Go for it."

Lily grasped the blood-soaked side of his shirt and lifted it up to expose his belly and ribs. There was considerable blood, all right, but there wasn't any more seeping out of him. Right before her eyes, the large, intensely painful gash in his side sealed itself into smooth, unmarred flesh still sticky with blood. She choked out a surprised breath and looked at him.

He smirked at her, still leaning against the wall. "Werewolf." His shirt dropped from her fingers, and she smacked him in the side instead. "Ow—hey."

"You let me worry about you until you were all healed up?"

"I heal really fast, yeah," he said and shied away from her with a chuckle. "The pain was real. It makes it kinda hard to think about anything else until it's over."

"Oh, hard to think is it? I thought I was gonna have to drive you to a hospital or something. Or somehow cast emergency healing spells I don't even—yeah. You just..." She raised her arms in exasperation, dropped them against her thighs again with a thump, and turned away to walk down the sidewalk.

"Hey, wait a minute." Romeo's laughter followed her,

and he grabbed her hand and yanked her around. She rolled her eyes until she realized how far he'd pulled her and how close she stood to him now. He held her hand against his chest, and she felt his other arm wind around her lower back to press her against him completely. She couldn't have fought against it even if she wanted to. "It's really good to know you would've tried to heal me," he said. "If you had to."

Lily looked at him and pursed her lips. "Don't make me have to. Deal?"

He grinned. "Absolutely."

She stared into his eyes and bit her lip. "Okay, you have to tell me right now if you—"

Romeo leaned down to kiss her, and the rest of her thought melted out of her brain when he brought both hands up to cup her cheeks. Everything disappeared but the heat of his body against hers and his mouth and the dark, earthy smell of him. She clutched his shirt in both fists and kissed him in return with enough force to pin him against the brick wall again. A low hum of approval vibrated from his lips into hers before she reined it in enough to pull back and exhale a long breath.

"If I what?" he asked softly and his breath whispered over her skin.

"Well..." Her chuckle sounded breathless. "I'm sure you just told me." He ran his fingers through her hair and made the back of her neck tingle. "If we hadn't recently crashed a major witch party, I'd tell you not to stop. But I think..." She shrugged

"Yeah, we should get outta here."

"Yeah." When he released her, she stepped back and looked at him. "Raincheck?"

He laughed. "I'm gonna hold you to that. Come on." Romeo grabbed her hand again, and they walked swiftly down the sidewalk on Boulevard de Maisonneuve.

There were still many cars out on the street and music played from the bars they passed. "Well, at least we know that if Black Suit and his bouncer goons try anything now, they'd expose themselves in the open. Front-row seats to a real-life magic show."

"Black Suit?"

"Oh. Yeah, the guy whose pants I set on fire."

Romeo chuckled. "I enjoyed that."

"Still, I'm not trying to hurt people. If he tries something, he's gonna need a witch who can handle memory wipes for a large crowd. That takes time. All we have to do is be quick, get out of Montreal, and disappear before the guy can recover enough to come after us."

"Yep. It seems doable."

Lily felt much better about their chances when they reached the RV in the parking garage without encountering any other witches. As far as she could tell with a quick sweep—and asking Romeo if his convenient sense of smell picked up any lingering magic—no one had connected their presence to the Winnebago before they could make their great escape. "Don't get me wrong. I love this thing but it's not really the best getaway car." She climbed into the driver's seat and started the engine.

Romeo sat beside her, strapped his seatbelt on, and pulled his phone out. "Yeah, but there are no hotel charges and no paper trail to follow. Nobody standing behind the welcome desk for anyone to bribe for information about where we went and what room we're in."

Lily stared at him. "It sounds like you've had some personal experience with this part."

With a shrug, he merely said, "I've watched enough detective shows to know it's possible."

"Okay, then." Smiling, Lily shook her head and backed the RV slowly out of the parking place. "Any ideas where to not get a hotel room tonight?"

"Actually...Mont Tremblant National Park is only two hours away."

"There's no way you reserved a campsite there, too."

He chuckled. "I'd have to be able to see the future for that. But I'm sure we can find a place somewhere close to pull over for the night. We can go find whatever we're supposed to find there in the morning. It's better than trying to stay here, right?"

"Yeah, being ambushed in the city doesn't sound all that great. So where to, then, navigator?"

"All right. We're gonna head out of here onto Autoroute 15. Turn right out of the garage and take the first left."

TWENTY

Once they were out on the highway and heading north to the national park, it seemed like a better time to ask a few questions. "For the sake of brainstorming," Lily said and focused her gaze on the road illuminated by the Winnie's headlights, "do you have any ideas why the owner of that wacko magical club would set an alarm for a keyring charm? Because I have no idea why it would be that important."

"I don't think it was the maple leaf."

"What do you mean?"

"Think about it. You stole his keys, too."

"Oh. Right. Hey, do you think my mom wanted me to take the keys instead of the charm?"

He put his hands behind his head, leaned back in the passenger seat, and hummed in thought. "Dunno. What do the keys look like?"

"They're in my purse." When he didn't move or say

anything else, she glanced at him briefly before returning her attention to the road. "What?"

"You're gonna let me go through your purse? Wait, you want me to go through your purse?"

"It's not gonna bite you. And if there was anything I wanted to hide from you, I definitely wouldn't put it in my purse and carry it around with me all the time."

"Are you sure there's not anything you wanna hide from me?"

Lily laughed. "Look, if you're fishin' for something, you're in the wrong lake." He snorted. "Oh, man. I sounded like your dad right there, didn't I?"

"If you scratch the super Southern accent, yeah. He would have said exactly that." Romeo leaned over the center console and retrieved her purse before setting it in his lap. He located the keys and only looked at them for a few seconds. "These are house keys."

"You just picked them up. How do you know they're house keys?"

"Well, they're definitely not car keys and there's nothing for a padlock or a safe. I guess they could be keys to any kind of building."

"Okay, besides a visitor center, how many buildings are there in a national park that need keys?"

He opened his mouth, closed it, and looked at the keyring again. "Dunno. But I bet you could do that tracking spell again once we get there. It worked to find these."

"I guess. It might be the best place to start— as long as I

don't get taken out Wicked-Witch-of-the-West style with a whole house landing on my head. Tracking spells can go both ways."

That seemed to end the brainstorming session for a few minutes until he dropped the keys into her purse and set it on the cupholders in the center console again. "Okay, I have a question for you, now."

"Go for it."

"Have you ever heard of a werewolf who could cast spells?"

That made her turn to look at him, and she almost forgot she was driving. He raised his eyebrows and twisted his mouth in confusion like he was apologizing for even asking. "Uh...not that I know of. That's not saying much, though, when the Council's spent centuries trying to wipe out any history about werewolves to keep witches from finding out that you aren't all simply a group of—" She swallowed.

"What, wild animals?"

"That's hard to say out loud."

"Really?"

"Yeah."

"Well, okay." Romeo ran a hand through his curly hair. "Everything I know essentially separates werewolves from magic altogether, except for being able to smell it. We can't cast spells, and we don't really add energy to rituals or however that works. But I..." He frowned and shifted to face her in the passenger seat. "Did you get a good look at the giant guy who punched me in the face?"

She snorted. "That's funny."

"It's funny that he punched me?"

"What? No." She cleared her throat. "I'm sorry. No, the way you said it. I mostly only saw the back of him. He did turn, but I blasted him across the room. So, no. Not really a good look. But I saw your eyes change after he hit you, so if anyone's trying to find us after this, they know you're a werewolf."

"Yeah, I know. So is he."

"What?" She shot him another quick glance. "Werewolves can't cast spells. And I saw both those guys throw green bolts more than once."

Romeo sighed. "Yep. That's what got me punched in the gut, too."

"You're gonna have to explain that one a little more."

"I saw his eyes change, Lily. First, he cast spells like a regular witch, then he punched me in the face. I reacted, and he actually growled at me, which was weird. But then his eyes went silver, which was even weirder and shouldn't have been possible 'cause he was using magic. So yeah, it surprised me, and I got punched in the stomach."

"Huh." She frowned at the glow of her headlights on the highway.

"So no ideas?"

Lily shrugged. "Maybe it was another spell? If you think about it, there are hundreds of different kinds, so it could've been the way he cast it that made his eyes look funny."

"That's what I thought at first, too. But I know what it

looks like when a wolf's about to show up. I swear that's what happened even though I can't understand how that's even possible." Romeo thumped his head back against the headrest and scratched behind his ear.

"So we'll keep that on the back burner," she said. "Who knows? Maybe we'll end up in a giant library of magical information and we'll find something about it there."

He tipped his head toward her and raised an eyebrow. "Does a library like that actually exist?"

"Well, yes. A few, actually. None of them are in Canada, though." She turned to shoot him a tight smile. "And in all my training and my mom's lessons, magical history never managed to keep my attention. You have no idea how boring it is."

"I might have a fairly good idea."

"Oh, yeah?" She laughed. "Did your dad lay out lesson plans and make you read all the historical accounts of werewolves?"

Romeo already knew she was joking. "No. No reading and no lessons. At least, not on paper. We spent hours in the woods, though."

"Hey, that's not boring. If my mom had taken me out into the woods for hands-on history lessons, I definitely would've paid more attention. Honestly, that was the only thing she didn't seem too interested in, either." Lily snorted. "When she left for her trips, she also left me magical history homework to do on my own."

He laughed and shook his head. "I literally meant that

I almost failed every history class in high school. That's the boring part."

"Oh. I failed math junior year."

"You?" He opened his mouth wide and exaggerated a ridiculous amount of shock.

"I know. I generally got good grades all round."

"So what happened with math junior year?" When he slammed his elbow down on the center console, he leaned toward her to prop his chin on his fist and fix her with a demanding stare.

"It's not that exciting. Actually, it was stupid,." She sighed and shook her head. "I forgot we had this big test coming up, so I didn't study for it. I was really nervous, and I didn't even think about it. I kinda leaned over to check what this girl Martha had put down for one of the prob- lems..." She shrugged

"You got caught cheating on a math test."

"You know, it doesn't actually sound any better when you say it out loud like that."

He laughed. "I'm totally surprised. You used to get pissed when I cheated at cards."

"And Scrabble. And dominoes."

"You can't cheat at dominoes."

Lily straightened against the back of the driver's seat and released a huge sigh. "Okay, fine. Maybe not domi- noes. And I only got pissed because those games are like... competitions. There's something to be gained from outsmarting the person you're playing against, right? And you're almost as smart as I am, so we were evenly matched." She gave him a sidelong look and hoped he caught on.

Romeo snorted. "Okay, smartypants. So, cheating at a game is way worse than cheating on a high school test because?"

"Romeo, when it came down to all the things I was learning and everything my mom was teaching me...in the big scheme of things, none of those tests really mattered. I'm not saying it was okay. I wasn't thinking, and yeah, I got caught. I'm not trying to argue against consequences for that or anything. But I never learned a thing studying for a school test that helped me with anything in my life after graduation." When she finished, the RV was uncomfortably quiet. She glanced at Romeo and leaned toward him. "That's it."

"That's actually exactly how I feel about all of it, Lil. I can't argue with that answer." He leaned back in his seat again and shrugged. "It makes sense."

"Hey, we've been on the same page for a long, long time, haven't we?"

"Yeah. It's actually amazing. Wait, how'd you fail math for cheating on one test?"

Lily scrunched her face. "Please don't make me say it."

"Is it really that bad?"

She glanced at him. "Kind of. And it's humiliating."

"Everybody makes mistakes, Lily."

"I don't think it's that normal to fail a math class for cheating on the math final, though."

Romeo barked out a laugh. "You forgot about a final?"

"Yeah."

"Like end of the year, it's almost summer so everybody has to study their ass off to get through it? That kinda final?"

"Yes. That kind of final. I told you it's humiliating. I was still trying to work out how to juggle high school with normal kids on one hand and all my mom's puzzles and training on the other. It kinda happened."

Romeo hissed a sigh through his teeth and shook his head. "You're somethin'."

"Oh, am I?"

"Yeah. I like it."

She smirked through the windshield and raised a shoulder. "Well, thank you. That's something we can work with."

AFTER A LITTLE UNDER an hour on Autoroute 15, they found signs for a rest area with bathrooms, food, drinking water, a gas station, and—most importantly, as Romeo didn't hesitate to point out—a legal place for them to park the Winnie while they slept. Lily was only too glad to pull off the highway and call it a night. "There's definitely such a thing as too much driving," she said and nodded at the three parked semis with their lights off and the engines cut. "I don't know how those guys do it—sleeping in those tiny beds up top. They get up super-early, don't they?"

"Yeah, probably. Catch all the daylight and everything."

She parked the Winnie in the designated area. They stood and took a minute to shake off the drive despite how short it was. "So," he said before a massive yawn. "It's been kind of a long, weird day, huh?" He knocked his shoes off against the top stair and kicked them against the back of the passenger seat.

"That's one way to put it." Lily raised her arms over her head, bent sideways, and sighed when her ribcage stretched in response. Once she'd repeated it on the other side, she lowered her arms and nodded. "I don't really feel like searching for hookups here. If there even are any. Are you okay with no power for the night? I can turn the generator on if you really want some air." He opened the side door and took a deep breath of the fresh mountain air outside.

"Nah. We can open all the windows. It's actually cool up here at night."

"Huh. Cold air in the middle of the summer. That's about as far from home as it can get, right?" She turned and opened the windows over the back of the couch, then stepped a few feet to the left and reached for the one behind the tiny kitchen table. "Oh, this one's stuck. I guess that's what I get for never opening the windows in this thing. It's not really the best choice at home, though." Romeo successfully opened the two windows beside the kitchen counter while she struggled with the last one. When it finally moved, she almost fell forward onto the kitchen table.

A second after she caught herself, his hands settled on her hips. She jumped and had to laugh at herself. "You really shouldn't sneak up on me like that." She would have turned to face him if he hadn't lowered his head close to her ear. Before he even said anything, a tiny, warm shiver rippled down her spine.

"You know what I'd really like to do right now?" He didn't whisper it, but his voice was so low, he might as well have.

"I think I could take a few guesses."

"Okay, maybe I phrased that a little wrong."

"You know, it's totally okay to admit it if you phrased it exactly the way you meant to." She grinned.

His hands slid over her hips and across her stomach until he'd wrapped his arms around her. He pulled her gently against him and nestled his chin in the dip between her neck and her shoulder.

Lily grinned when she realized she'd automatically settled her own arms over his. *Like we've always fit together this way*. She squeezed his forearms and tilted her head to make a little more room for his cheek next to hers. "So phrasing it differently, then," she said, "what is it you wanna do right now?"

"Well, I try not to make a habit of inviting myself into a girl's bed right after escaping angry witches in an underground circus and kissing her for the first time."

"Well, yeah. That would be a hard habit to form in the first place."

"But I'm going to anyway. Maybe it's weird, but I really wanna sleep with you."

She laughed and tried to lean far enough away from him to look at his face. "You do, huh?"

"I mean literally sleep, okay?" Chuckling, he released her from the circle of his arms and turned her to face him. He settled his hands on her hips again as he smiled down at her. "Just next to you. I won't try anything, I promise." Lily widened her eyes and bit back another laugh. "Unless you want me to," he added quickly and closed his eyes. "All of that sounded better in my head, by the way."

She cradled his face with both hands and pulled him down gently for a short, soft kiss. When she drew away, his eyes were still closed. "Honestly, I'm exhausted." He looked at her and bit his lip through a smile. "So if you mean literally sleep and that's it, I totally accept your invitation. Into my bed."

Romeo grinned. "Cool."

"Cool." She took his hand, studied him for a minute longer, and turned and led him through the narrow space to her room in the back of the Winnebago. *Well, it's unexpected but feels totally natural. The first time I bring him to my room is in this Winnebago. That's kinda cool.* She slid the thin paneled door open. *I guess there's a first time for everything.* When they stood at the foot of the bed, she released his hand. "So."

He glanced at her, turned, and spread his arms before he fell back and flopped onto the covers. Shaking her head, Lily stepped out of her flats, turned off the lights, and crawled onto the bed beside him. "I have no idea if I'm a cover hog or not, so be prepared." She flipped back the comforter she'd never fully made up and shoved her legs under it.

Romeo copied her perfectly, even when she lay on her

side and propped her head on her hand. "Don't worry about me." He batted his eyelids and gave her the goofiest, closed-lipped smile.

"Oh, I'm not."

When he rolled over onto his back and opened his arms, she couldn't say no to snuggling against him under the covers and resting her head on his chest. "Hey, this is kinda like all the nights we spent in our sleeping bags in a tent. Or that cabin in Edisto."

Romeo chuckled. "I think the only way this is kinda like that is that I'm happy."

"Aww..." She tipped her head back to look at him. "Things haven't really been the easiest for the last little while, huh? I mean for both of us."

"That's a gentle representation of the truth, I think." He bent his arm to rub her back lightly.

"I only mean that this"—she draped her arm across his chest and settled her ear over his heart to listen to its slow, steady rhythm—"feels easy. It's always been easy with you." She felt him look at her, so she tipped her head up and almost laughed at his wide-eyed expression.

"The cuddling was implied, though, right?"

She smiled and settled her cheek onto his chest. "Yes, it was." A few seconds later, she drifted off to sleep with the slow rise and fall of his chest beneath her. This was sweet and safe and simple.

THE BLACK SHADOW of a bird floated through the Canadian night sky, searching. When it found the vehicle at the rest stop on Autoroute 15, it dove through the metal roof once again to complete its purpose. But when it relayed the image of the young witch sleeping in the werewolf's arms, it was called back to wait for a better opportunity.

TWENTY-ONE

When she stirred out of sleep the next morning, Lily rolled over in bed and flopped her arm out onto the pillow beside her.

"Ow—hey," the pillow groaned.

She bolted upright and blinked at Romeo who rubbed his temple and squinted at her. "Oh." She put her hands to her mouth to hold her laughter back, but it didn't quite work. "I'm sorry. I...totally forgot you were there."

He propped himself up on his elbow and squinted against the sunlight coming through the bedroom window. "It's nice to know I left such a good impression."

"You know that's not the way I meant it." Her face felt tight when she rubbed it and she gave her cheeks a little pat. "Time to go find out what the maple leaf is for, right?"

Romeo wrinkled his nose at her and tilted his head with a hesitant smile. "I don't think I've ever seen you wake up on the right side of the bed before."

Lily shrugged. "Maybe it's the mountain air. Come on.

Do you think Canada's gas-station breakfast is any better than ours?"

She managed to find old-fashioned oats and a tiny carton of one-percent milk. With the gas station's microwave and a little maple syrup from the coffee cart, she enjoyed a breakfast that dealt with her hunger but wouldn't sit like a leaden lump in her stomach for the rest of the day. Romeo insisted on paying for it with his bacon, egg, and cheese breakfast sandwich. She bought the coffee.

The next hour of driving up Autoroute 15 N would take them into Mont Tremblant National Park. After that, she had no idea what they were supposed to do, but they had various things they could try.

Romeo spent ten minutes looking on his phone for the next song he wanted to play. When the music finally started, she almost sprayed her mouthful of coffee over the steering wheel. She had to swallow hard before saying anything at all. "Lonely Island?"

"What? It could work. Trade 'boat' for 'RV,' and it's basically the same thing." He took a long sip of his own coffee and paused in thought. "Or maybe we start calling this a boat."

"Not even close."

"Are you sure?"

She looked away from the road long enough to say, "No mermaids."

He snorted.

It DIDN'T SEEM weird that they'd been up and ready to go at something close to seven in the morning, which had to be the case as they stopped at the entrance of the national park at 8:17 a.m.

They didn't have a reservation for a campsite, so they pulled the RV up to one of the dirt parking lots at the trailhead that eventually split into four different hiking trails, according to the sign. "This is probably as far in as we can go in the Winnie, right?" Lily asked as she turned the engine off.

"Probably. That means more hikes for us." He wiggled his eyebrows and unbuckled his seatbelt.

"Hopefully without any partying witch covens or dudes named Kevin."

"I'd be seriously impressed if we found both or even either of those here. Maybe a little creeped out, too."

She dropped her keys into her purse, then thought better of it and took them out again. "Okay. Here we go. I have two sets of keys and a plan for a tracking spell."

"And me." He nudged her to make his point.

"Well, that goes without saying."

Once she'd locked the RV and blinked against the morning sun already fairly high in the sky, she retrieved the keys they'd commandeered from the back pocket of her jean shorts and tossed and caught them in her hand a few times. "So, if I do this tracking spell right now, we need a plan."

Romeo adjusted the straps of his pack on his shoulders.

He'd emptied and refilled it with water bottles, a blanket, and a collection of stuff he said was good to have just in case. "You mean besides follow the purple light?"

She shifted her weight onto one foot. "I mean a plan for if anyone sees us. You know. National park, morning hikers, and the high probability that anyone we run into isn't a witch."

"Thinking ahead. I like it." He pointed at her, rubbed his hands together, and looked at the maple-leaf charm attached to the technically stolen keyring. "But I think we've become good at improvising. I wanna see this magical tracking device."

"Wow. You're way more into this than I expected."

"Come on, Lil. I love watching you do your thing."

"Okay." She glanced around them at the trailhead, although the RV essentially blocked them from the view of anyone who might pass on the road. She cast the same spell she'd used in the office—a tap on the leaf charm and a line drawn from left to right in the air.

"Where's the purple line?" Romeo frowned at the air between them and glanced quickly at her.

"I...don't know. Lemme try again." Clearing her throat, she shook her hand, rolled her shoulders back, and ran through the motions and the intention once again with no result. "So what's the deal, here? We put the two pieces together. There was a big flash, the metal leaf shocked me, but now, apparently, there's nothing here to link it to where we're trying to go. And there has to be a purpose for this keyring. My mom wouldn't have left it for me for fun."

"Um..." He gestured at her hand and mimed turning a

key in a lock. "Maybe it's not the charm she wanted you to follow."

"Why not? She left me half of it."

"Yeah, and the other half was attached to those keys. So maybe the key goes to something here, and that's where she wanted you to end up."

Lily stared at him in confusion. "I thought we already covered the fact that a house key—or a building key—won't open anything in the middle of a national park."

"Lily, try it." He shrugged and spread his arms. "It's obvious that nothing bad happens if it doesn't work."

"Except for me knowing that it didn't work." She blew out a heavy breath and tried again. But when the spell didn't work on the first key, she dropped her hands to her thighs with a muffled jingle. "This is stupid."

"Three keys, Lily. So where's the door for key number two?" Shooting her the guns with both hands might've been the only thing to make her chuckle in that moment.

"Let it be...really close." Her fingertip touched the grooved teeth of the key, and she drew a quick line in the air from left to right before she flung her hand toward the forest in resignation. She did not expect the purple line to leave a blazing trail after her finger and streak down the trailhead at her flippant gesture.

"Yes!" Romeo pumped a fist. "We have our tracker."

"You are...actually really good at pep talks." She grinned at him. "Let's see where it goes." She stepped past him onto the trail and glanced over her shoulder. "Thanks for the key suggestion."

"Hey, with great suggestions comes great responsibility. I gotcha."

———

"I DON'T KNOW if it's normal for the trails to be so empty, but I'm glad we haven't seen anybody yet. It makes following this purple line much easier right now." The path of her spell basically followed the literal path along which they walked. When the trail split again to take them either left or right, the glowing purple line stretched on directly ahead, off the trail and into the woods.

"Okay, I can handle hikes," Lily said. "But I'm not sure I'm down to wander off the trail in a huge national park. People get seriously lost doing that."

"Most people don't have me with them." Romeo stopped beside her and peered through the tall coniferous trees after the purple light. "Or a werewolf in general." He looked at her and nodded. "I can get us back."

She studied him for a few seconds, after which he offered her a patient smile. "Right. I'm gonna let you handle this one."

"Please do." He stepped aside and gestured for her to lead the way following her spell. She stepped off the path and into the underbrush, and he crunched after her.

She'd forgotten how much fun it was to blaze through a forest without following someone else's guidelines for where to step and how far to go. The birds were so much louder in the denser trees off the path and the air cooler with more shade and perhaps a little more humid without an unrestrained breeze. Following the purple tracker meant she didn't have to think about where she was going other than to step over the occasional fallen log covered in moss or skirt around what could have been a hole buried under rotting, untouched leaves from the previous fall. The deeper they moved through the forest, away from cities and roads and people, the more she daydreamed about spending all her time out there like this. "You know, I wouldn't mind bringing the Winnie out here to a place like this and kinda hanging out for a while."

"I wouldn't mind joining you."

She shrugged. "That could be arranged."

Half an hour later, the woods opened onto a decent-sized lake—nothing massive, but it was enough to light up the shallow valley with the sunshine that reflected off the water. That was where the purple trail of her tracking spell ended.

"What?" Lily stared out over the lake, then turned in a slow circle and tried to find the snaking glow that had led them there.

"A spell like that doesn't have a shelf life, does it?" Romeo sounded equally as confused.

"No. When it ends, it means we're where we need to be. So now I'd like to know why a key led us to the edge of a lake in the middle of nowhere."

"Wait a minute." His head jerked to the side and he sniffed the air.

"If you're gonna say you smell magic, I want you to remember that you may also be smelling mine."

He looked at her, shook his head, and sniffed again. "No, it's not yours."

"You mean you can smell the difference between two different witches' magic?"

"Oh, yeah. Hold on." He walked in a few wide circles farther and farther to her left, constantly sniffing the air with a pause here and there. "What the—" A loud thump was immediately followed by, "Oh, come on."

"Is everything okay over there?" She turned to frown at him but he grinned like he'd found buried treasure.

"Better than okay. Watch." He stooped to pick up a handful of small pebbles and tossed them into the air. They didn't go far or complete the usual arc one would expect. Instead, they bounced off a surface that wasn't visible and some of them pattered back against his chest as if he'd tossed them at—

"A wall?" Lily asked and stepped toward him. "You found an invisible wall?"

"Or an invisible house. Right?" He wiggled his eyebrows at her and reached out to pat what neither of them could see. He must've misjudged the distance, but he corrected his little stumble and stepped tentatively forward before he managed to pat what could only be an invisible wall.

"I am so glad you came with me on this trip." She stopped behind him and put her hands on her hips as she attempted to study the surface of something she couldn't see. "Is there any chance you know a revealing spell or two?"

"Spells are your thing."

"Yes. I simply tried to be open to possibilities." Lily bit her lip and fumbled in her back pocket again for the keyring. Knowing the right spell wasn't necessary at this point. The minute she separated the key that had led them here from the others, the view of the forest in front of them was replaced by a small log cabin.

"But you wouldn't have needed anyone else's spells at all." Romeo nodded at the lock on the door, and it would've been completely ridiculous not to try the key. It fit, of course, and it turned in the lock with one fluid motion.

The door opened into a dark, musty, one-room cabin. "I'd say it's a little weird that the key led us here. But all the magical work went into hiding the outside. There isn't much left over for sprucing up."

The far wall held a tall bookshelf with a selection of jars stacked in neat rows. The items inside looked like pickles or maybe canned peppers until a second glance revealed a disturbing likeness to severed fingers. Lily didn't look again to double-check. A fireplace and a cookstove stood on the far right wall, a small table and two chairs in the middle of the room, a few more shelves of cooking utensils and random tools along the other wall, and a single bed nestled in the far left corner. Beside that was an old wooden trunk, and that completed the invisible cabin in the woods.

Each wall had one high, square window, all of them shuttered, but the wooden slats were old and warped. Some sunlight spilled through, but it wasn't nearly enough light to search thoroughly to find whatever her mom had left for her. Lily closed the door behind them and summoned a bright orb of yellow light. She raised it until it elevated on its own and hovered in the center of the ceiling like a helium balloon. "Okay. If I were Greta Antony, where would I leave the treasure chest? One clue led us to the magical speakeasy. The other led us here..." Her gaze fell onto the trunk at the foot of the bed, and she nodded her head thoughtfully. "Actually, it might actually be that blatantly obvious."

"The trunk?" Romeo asked.

"Yeah, why not? We already deciphered the hardest parts. She taught me a lot about looking where no one else would think to look, but Mom's always been a fan of 'hidden in plain sight.'" The trunk was unlocked and quite easy to open despite the heavy wooden lid. On the underside of the lid, she found her namesake burned into the lighter wood—a lily blossom on a long stem. "Oh, this is totally it."

The trunk, though, was almost completely empty. The only thing inside was a tiny parcel wrapped in brown butcher paper—no string, no tape, merely wrapped and crumpled up. "And she would definitely have wrapped anything important in something like this. If anyone else found it, they'd think it was a piece of trash."

"Isn't it?"

"No." Lily snatched the small parcel and sat on the dusty bedcover, and the mattress springs squeaked beneath her weight. The butcher paper was dusty and brittle, but it came away quickly to reveal a tiny, thumb-sized mirror in a silver frame strung on a silver necklace chain and a note.

Her breath caught in her throat when she unfolded the

small square of paper. She stopped breathing altogether when she recognized her mom's handwriting, but she forced herself to keep going.

YOU'VE NEVER NEEDED *anyone to do anything for you, sweets. And you never will. But remember how important it is to find those people who will drop everything to do something with you. Especially when you don't need them.*

If you ever find yourself running out of options, try looking backward to unravel the most powerful setback.

Ask Bentley about 452.

SHE STARED at the short note and read it over one more time.

"What does it say?"

"Only Greta-speak for 'empower yourself, Lily.' It's probably another clue. And a tiny mirror on a necklace." She held it out in her palm, and Romeo leaned forward for a quick look.

His gaze drifted into the open trunk. "Uh...I think you missed something." He leaned forward to stretch inside it and retrieved a brown leather coin purse that jingled in his fist. "If it was anyone but your mom, seeing this right now wouldn't make any sense at all."

Lily scoffed and nodded at the bag. "What's in it?"

He fiddled with the drawstring for a moment, opened the purse, and peered inside. His eyes grew incredibly wide. "Gold."

"Yeah, but what kind of—wait, what?"

"Literally. Gold coins."

"Oh, my God." She leapt up from the squeaky bed and peered into the open bag that rested in his palm.

"How much do you think's in there?"

"I have no idea. We'll have to get it appraised...somewhere. There are gold and diamond brokers everywhere."

He sniggered. "An actual treasure chest."

Lily slipped the silver chain with the mirror over her head, where it settled perfectly below her throat, and stuffed her mom's note into her front pocket. "Mission accomplished. Let's get back to the Winnie, huh?"

"Well, okay." They crossed the room toward the cabin's only door, and Lily let him gape at the bag of gold coins in his hand for a little while longer. She could go through it herself when they were back on the road again, and she actually really enjoyed the way his eyes glittered simply to see so much of it in one place.

She was about to take hold of the doorknob when his other hand snaked out to grab her wrist with frightening speed. "Wait." He sniffed the air a few times and turned slowly to meet her gaze.

"You're kidding me," she whispered.

"Someone's here."

TWENTY-TWO

The second after he said those words, the shutters on all four windows flew open. Sunlight streamed into the cabin. "I assume that's not to set the mood," Lily whispered.

Romeo sniffed again. "Three of them."

"Right. So the plan is to—"

A green, swirling ball of light burst through the window on their right, followed shortly by one more through each of the other windows. She dragged him into a crouch beside her and stared at the pulsing orbs. They converged on each other and joined slowly in the center of the cabin to make one much greater sphere in the air.

"I can take at least one of them if we get outside first," Romeo said. "Probably two."

"For now, stay right here with me. I need to focus for...I dunno. It should only take a couple of seconds." He nodded. "Actually, this is really weird to see one of my mom's training spells being used against me for real.

It's a good thing I learned about this one a long time ago." Her fingers twitched at her sides as she watched the growing green mass above them pulse and swell, bigger and brighter. "It's all in the timing. I only gotta wait for the—"

The second her eyes registered the telltale flash, her instincts and training kicked in. She raised both hands and created a warded shield, making sure to think about Romeo too. The ensuing explosion of green light and the force of the spell pounded against her raised shield and crackled like a lightning bolt striking the roof of a car. It wiped her mind completely blank for those first few seconds.

"What is this?" Romeo shouted over the noise.

"Huh?" She turned to look at him but kept her hands raised and pushed back against the attack spell with slightly more force. "Right. It's like a magical flash grenade but a little more intense."

"Oh." He nodded like he understood all of it completely, but he looked confused and way too skeptical.

"And it lasts longer," she said and raised her voice over the green, roaring magic that pummeled her shields nonstop. "So while we have a minute, I remembered something."

"Oh, yeah?"

"I know you can heal super-fast. Is there anything that...you know. Does the job? Permanently?"

"Are you trying to ask me how a werewolf can be killed?"

Lily nodded and licked her lips. "Yup."

"An aggressive amount of unrelenting metal."

She looked at him blankly for a moment. "You mean a bullet?"

"Lots of bullets."

That statement was followed by an almost deafening silence when the magical flash grenade finally fizzled out. "This is the part where they think we're...incapacitated," she whispered. "It might be the best time to open the door."

He glanced across the cabin and nodded, and they stooped low beneath the view of the windows to shuffle the few steps to the entrance. He took hold of the doorknob and she mouthed a count to three. The door burst open faster than she could see and Romeo vanished. A shout of surprise rose directly outside, followed by a ferocious snarl and a man's scream. Lily had a ball of fire in one hand a flare of red sparking in the other before her feet touched the pebbles at the edge of the lake.

She felt the magic more than heard it, which was enough to make her duck under a bright blue net of sizzling energy. It landed somewhere behind her instead, but she didn't hesitate to hurl the fireball at whatever witch had attacked her. The man behind the energy net deflected her spell with a quick wave. It was Black Suit, only he'd switched to black jeans and a black t-shirt.

"Nice try," he spat.

Lily hurled her stronger attack at him, but he zapped it with what looked like a neon-blue tentacle that erupted from his finger and rendered her attempt completely useless. "Wait, what did you—"

"You know," Black Suit said as he stalked toward her

and summoned the sharp, slicing yellow spell in his hand again, "I don't remember inviting you out here."

"Nope. Someone else did." She brought another round of angry red sparks to crackle at her fingertips and waited. The man narrowed his eyes and tilted his head to study her belligerently.

"Who are you?"

She wanted to laugh, but that was probably pushing it. "You know, I'm still trying to work that part out." Then she decided she could forget the sparks and repeat the unintentional black cloud she'd set off in Le Chapeau Magique. She clapped her hands but grunted when huge, sweaty arms wound around her from behind and squeezed to pin her hands in front of her.

"You won't use that one again," her captor snapped in her ear. "It took us five hours to clear all the damage."

"That's a little slow, don't you think?" She stamped on the man's foot and drove her elbow into his gut at the same time, expecting him to either double over or release her completely. A black, streaking blur bolted from around the side of the cabin and launched itself at the man before he could react. Both her attacker and the wolf who'd pounced on top of him rolled across the pebbly beach toward the lake. "You got it?" she shouted at Romeo. "Yeah, you got it. And you can't answer me. Okay."

Taking advantage of the situation, she stepped quickly toward Black Suit and clapped her hands again. He glared at her, reached back, and drew a gun from the waistband of his jeans. In one swift motion, he swung his arm wide and took aim—not at Lily but at the lake.

The gunshot and Lily's scream echoed out over the water at the same time, followed by a piercing, yelping bark. The man who'd been pinned beneath the black wolf's massive paws and snapping jaw two seconds before shoved the huge beast off. Romeo rolled into the clear water of the beach and the waves lapping gently at the shore, completely limp.

"It looks like you're on your own, now." Black Suit sniggered and nodded at his one remaining man out of the two he'd brought with him. "Let's get her back. I want her in a room that'll make her a little more...open to answering questions." His brown eyes glistened in the sunlight when his gaze fell on Lily again. "I want to know everything you know."

Lily's chest heaved, but she couldn't let herself fall apart now. "Not gonna happen," she said through clenched teeth. *Keep talking and buy yourself time to come up with something.* "That's a cheap trick bringing a gun to a witch fight."

He tucked the firearm into the back of his jeans again and glanced at the edge of the lake. "Well, it worked."

And that seemed to be her limit when it when it came to thinking of ways to stall. At this point, she was reasonably sure she'd run out of options.

If you ever find yourself running out of options, try looking backward to unravel the most powerful setback.

The line from her mom's note flashed through her head, and she froze for a moment. *Okay, okay. Look backward, Lily. What's the most powerful setback? What do you need right now?*

Romeo.

Her hand shot up to clutch the tiny mirror dangling from the silver chain.

"What's she doing?" Black Suit's goon grumbled.

His boss stared at her, and one of his eyes twitched. "She's stalling."

"Please, please, please. Unravel it. Come on."

The mirror in her hand flashed silver, then gold, and a tingling warmth rushed through it into her fingers and up her arm. She ran to the edge of the water and searched the shoreline for the furry black body that might or might not have changed back into the person without whom she'd just realized she couldn't do any of this. Not because she literally couldn't but because she didn't want to.

In a handful of seconds, she knew Romeo's body was gone. Only that didn't make sense, because bodies didn't simply disappear, no matter what shape they took. She whirled away from the beach. "Where is he?" she shouted. "What did you—"

Black Suit and his hired thug were gone too, just like that. No spell shimmered in their wake and there had been no surprise attack or sound of pounding feet through the forest. They were all simply gone. Lily had just been in the middle of her first real duel—if she could even call it that— after being attacked in the parking garage back home and now, she was completely alone.

She sucked in a sharp, jagged breath and stared out over the sparkling water. "What do I do now?" Something splashed down the shore on her left, and her head whipped that way before she stumbled back. "What?"

A man trudged through the water and up onto the beach, dripping wet from head to toe and yes, completely naked. He flung his hands out with a spray of water across the pebbles, then stopped when he noticed her staring at him.

"This time, I'm just gonna tell you up front that I'm fine—"

A shout of surprise and relief escaped her and she raced across the beach toward him. Romeo grunted when she threw her arms around his neck and pressed her lips fiercely against his, clutching at his dripping hair. After a moment, she simply settled for hugging him because she couldn't catch her breath. "I thought you were dead. I thought...the gun...and you... How are you okay? He shot you."

"Yeah. Once."

"What?"

He raised his eyebrows and grinned. "I said lots of bullets. That was only one."

She laughed despite herself. "But it still got you. Why aren't you hugging me back? What's wrong?"

Romeo tilted his head and hunched his shoulders with a hesitant chuckle. "I'm naked."

"Oh." She released him and looked down without thinking to see him covering himself with both hands. Quickly jerking her gaze up to meet his, she stepped back. "Oh. Right."

"Yeah. So I'll uh...gimme a sec?" He nodded and headed farther up the beach toward the cabin but paused and looked around him. "Where'd everybody go?"

She had to drag her gaze to the back of his head as he walked buck-naked away from her. "Huh?"

"Did you take care of the other two? The witches?"

"I think so?" Her hand went to the mirror charm again.

"I'm officially impressed."

"You and me both. I'm not entirely sure what this thing did. But yeah. I guess I got 'em." When she looked toward the cabin, Romeo was gone again, and her heart fluttered in her chest. "Romeo?" She couldn't get back to the cabin fast enough. "Romeo!"

"Yeah." He stepped around the corner of the stacked logs, pulling his t-shirt over his head. "Are you okay?"

She puffed out a sigh of relief and smiled. "Definitely okay. Only a little jumpy, I think."

"Well..." He slung his trekking pack over his shoulder and stooped to grab something off the ground. "This'll make the day a little better, right?" Something clinked and jangled when he tossed it to her, and she snatched the brown purse of gold coins from the air.

"Yeah," she said slowly as she walked toward him and weighed the purse in her hand. "Like the cherry on top." She looked up at him and sighed. "But if I'd actually lost you today, I'd probably chuck this thing into the lake."

When she reached him, he put his arm around her and pulled her close, his shirt already a little damp. She didn't care. "That would be a really aggravating way to honor me."

Lily chuckled. "I'll settle for honoring the living. How bout that?"

"It sounds good. So, now that we've gotten a little bit closer, what's next?"

She stared at the bag of gold in her hand. "She actually left me a bag of gold. You know, I think I'll use this to finally rip all that carpet out of the Winnie," she said and stuffed it into her back pocket.

"Or maybe get that shower problem looked at, huh?"

Lily laughed, slipped her arm around his waist, and let him guide her back through the woods toward the trail. "If I do that, how am I supposed to get you shirtless and all soaped up?"

Romeo lowered his head toward her and grinned. "I promise, that is not the only way."

TWENTY-THREE

I t was time for lunch when they reached the Winnebago, but Lily couldn't force herself to think about food—or driving, for that matter. Romeo seemed entirely too ready to get back on the road. "I like Canada and everything," he said as he dropped his pack onto the floor and nudged it under the kitchen table with the toe of his shoe. "It's a little...weird, though."

"I think that's 'cause we didn't exactly set out for the ultimate tourist experience," she said and shuffled toward the driver's seat. She scowled at it and stepped aside when he slipped past her and eased behind the wheel instead.

"Whaddya say?" He spread his arms and looked expectantly at her.

She opened her mouth and took a deep breath. "I... think you earned it."

"Seriously?"

"Yeah."

"Don't worry, Lil. I'll take care of her." He held his

palm out and it took her a second to remember to pull her keys from her back pocket. As soon as he turned the engine on, the stereo pumped out a steadily rising drumbeat and electric guitar. "Hey." He nodded his head to the music. "You know, I think this is the one."

"What?" Lily pulled a face but couldn't help smiling at him. She leaned against the passenger seat and folded her arms. "I don't know what this is," she said seconds before the first line of Aerosmith's shouted lyrics came through.

He spread his arms. "Back in the saddle again, baby."

"Oh, you think this is our theme song?"

"Yes. It's perfect. Especially now, 'cause I get to drive this beast."

She unfolded her arms and stepped toward him. "So it's more like your theme song, then."

Holding her gaze, he smiled and spread his arms even wider. "I'm totally willing to share."

"But what if it's way better as my background music?" She stepped over the center console, swung her leg over his, and put her hands on his shoulders. "I think this started playing for me." She sat in his lap and ran her fingers through the hair at the back of his neck.

"Oh." He chuckled and grabbed her hips. "I see what you did there." Biting her lip, Lily merely shrugged and leaned toward him. "I still like sharing, though."

"Good." She pressed him back into the seat and leaned away enough to pull her shirt up over her head and toss it onto the dash. The fact that his eyes never once left hers, even then, made it impossible for her not to take his face in her hands and pull him toward her again for a long, deep kiss. His hands moved from her hips to her bare back, and she let herself go.

That afternoon in the parking lot of a Canadian national forest, they had all the time in the world. She was sure she'd worked out how to keep anything and everything from stopping her now.

WHEN THEY MADE it across the Canadian border again—with another of Lily's spells on a passport and most of the tension from their first border crossing released—she decided it was as good a time as any to give Bentley McClure one more call.

"That note from my mom," she said and glanced at Romeo. "It said to ask Bentley about 452."

"Then you have to ask him, right?"

The man sounded entirely surprised to hear from her when he answered the phone.

"Is everything okay?" he asked.

"Yeah, Bentley. I'm fine. We're safe and... Well, it turns out Mom did actually leave something for me up in Canada." She glanced at Romeo behind the wheel. "Part of that was a note that mentioned you."

There was a few seconds' pause and he cleared his throat. "Really?"

"Yeah. All it said was, 'Ask Bentley about 452.' Does that mean anything to you?"

Her mom's accountant released a deep sigh and chuckled. Lily was so surprised, she pulled the phone away from her ear to make sure she'd dialed the right number. "Your mother was a clever woman."

"I can't argue with you there. Do you have any idea what she meant?"

"Of course I do, Lily. I'm merely...I'm so glad you're safe."

"Me too. I promised I would be."

Romeo glanced at her, then returned his attention to the road. "What's he saying?"

Lily pulled her phone away from her mouth to say, "He knows what it means."

"Are you there?" Bentley asked.

"Yeah. I'm right here."

"Your mom has a wide network of magical friends. Looking for 452 will bring you in contact with quite a few of them, I imagine. And a few more magicals who...well, Greta put a lot of work into keeping her friends close. Do you know the rest of the saying?"

"And her enemies closer. I understand."

He cleared his throat. "If I were you, I'd write this down."

IN A METAL CAGE two miles underground, a woman sat on the cold stone floor and raised her face to the darkness. Her long blonde hair was matted with dust, dirt, and her own blood, but not enough of it had been spilled yet to stop her.

A single candle flickered on a wobbly wooden table beyond the cage. The woman had drawn the smoke from the flame to her for the last twenty-four hours and pulled all her energy into another spell. It was the only option they'd left her, and no one even knew. Not yet.

When her energy had renewed enough to try one more time—and she would likely try again, and again, until their time had completely run out—the woman centered herself and cast once more.

Her arms jerked out to her sides, spread as wide and as far as her muscles would allow. A long, hollow gasp escaped her throat, and she threw her head back in the darkness. The vision brought her everything she wanted to see, everything she needed to see, and she would not stop until she'd accomplished the one thing in this world that mattered the most.

The soot-blackened smoke burst from her body and launched itself through the earth above this cavern. It would rise into the sky and move across the world to wherever it needed to go. For this woman, failure was not an option.

When it was done, she only had the strength to whisper one word. "Lily."

Lily and Romeo have to follow the last clue to an unusual location. Find out what her mother has left for her at this new location as the road trip continues in Witch Way To Go!

Get sneak peeks, exclusive giveaways, behind the scenes content, and more.
PLUS you'll be notified of special **one day only fan pricing** on new releases.

Sign up today to get free stories.

CLICK HERE

or visit: https://marthacarr.com/read-free-stories/

For Hire: Teachers for special school in Virginia countryside.

Must be able to handle teenagers with special abilities.

Cannot be afraid to discipline werewolves, wizards, elves and other assorted hormonal teens.

Apply at the School of Necessary Magic.

AVAILABLE AT AMAZON RETAILERS

Find the compass, save the world or save herself?

Dating is harder for Maggie Parker than running down a felon. Now add in magic.

Did she just see a compass fly?

Can she learn how to use the magic of bubbles to chart a new course in time? It's a lot harder than it sounds.

Join her on her quest to rescue passengers on an ancient ship – a big blue marble called Earth – and save herself.

<u>AVAILABLE ON AMAZON AND IN KINDLE UNLIMITED!</u>

AUTHOR NOTES - MARTHA CARR

AUGUST 6, 2019

The author and Pulitzer Prize winner, Toni Morrison died today at 88. She was a voice and a force that encouraged others, in particular women to have conversations that are authentic and honest without crossing into preaching or judgment. But the lessons are really meant for all of us regardless of the descriptions we're born with or the ones we take on later.

I came from a chaotic family that used silence as a weapon, ignoring each other when the opinions didn't match the company line. By the time I was a young woman, I had a roaring current of words running through my head, but very little of it ever left the premises through my mouth. The affect left me feeling alone in a room full of people.

Fortunately, I started to write. My 'local' paper was The Washington Post and I didn't get that it was really a bigger stage when I submitted my first piece, which was accepted and printed. I had told some of the truth about myself and how I see the world and then I waited, somewhat scared, for the reactions from readers. My family was horrified that I had stepped out like that, but at the same time, another curious thing happened.

Not only did readers start to write to me with stories about their lives to thank me for my honesty, but friends of my parents started to write them with the same messages. Letters showing up in the mailbox from all over the country. To this day, I can see the look of surprise on my parents' faces; like the idea that being yourself no matter what, was even possible. It was in that moment that I set myself free because I gave myself permission to speak – more and more and more.

I got to know the world and the world got to know me. That love affair is still going on and it changed my life for the better in a million little ways. It changed my son's life because I became a different parent. It changed the lives of everyone I come into contact with because I'm actually present. I'm listening and contributing the unique thing I bring to the table as well as celebrating whoever you are.

I let go of control over how things looked, what others thought, what it all meant and settled back into a different philosophy. The universe loves me, loves you – just as you are and therefore, I don't need to seek that love, to prove I'm worthwhile or become something else. I'm good, right here, as I am so I can go be of service, go have fun, go be curious about the world, instead.

It's a kind of forgiveness for just being human that allows in love and leaves me time to do other things – rather than wasting time trying to prove something that is static, never changes. That truth is that we are all born worthwhile, and we live that way with the same amount. We can't lose that worth, we won't get more, it's the same as everyone else.

In honor of Ms. Morrison and the gifts she gave the world, I'm going to step up my game and be myself a little more this week. It's the best kind of goal. We set the truth free and let it do its own work. More adventures to follow.

THANK YOU for not only reading this story but these *Author Notes* as well.

(I think I've been good with always opening with "thank you." If not, I need to edit the other *Author Notes*!)

RANDOM (*sometimes*) THOUGHTS?

If this is your first Judith Berens book, thank you SO much for reading, and you probably have no idea what's going on in these *Author Notes*.

Let me tell you a little about who I am.

I'm a guy who started writing a paranormal sci-fi series called *The Kurtherian Gambit* a little under four (4) years ago.

It was way more successful than I ever expected to be, and I used some of my success to help other authors. One of those efforts was talking about how I built a pretty successful series in just a few months on Amazon.

In the audience at that Austin meeting (of about eighty people) was Martha Carr, and a young author she had brought to see whether that Michael Anderle guy was the real deal.

She was one of three people to ask me questions after the event.

Now, three years later, we have a hugely successful universe together, multiple series in all sorts of genres, and we share some of our stories under the Judith Berens pen name.

If you get a chance, check out our first series (*The Leira Chronicles - Waking Magic* is the first book).

We didn't use a pen name for that series. It's just Martha and me!

AROUND THE WORLD IN 80 DAYS

One of the interesting (at least to me) aspects of my life is the ability to work from anywhere and at any time. In the future, I hope to re-read my own *Author Notes* and remember my life as a diary entry.

Paris, France—looking at the Eiffel Tower all lit up as I type this.

I have a secret I'm going to share a little later.

My job allows me a certain amount of freedom. I get to work from (almost) anywhere in the world where I have power and an internet connection.

Having the Eiffel Tower (all lit up at night) out my window is one such location.

That freedom is a digital noose. Stephen Campbell

(who runs the operations for the company) is able to ping me no matter where in the world I am and remind me I have *Author Notes* to write.

"Michael," he will type in Slack (our messaging platform) "You have four *Author Notes* due this week."

"But Steve," I'll respond (ok, it might sound like whining in my head, but that's only because I'm still jet-lagged and EVERYTHING that sounds like work makes me want to say ugly things in my head.)

I digress.

"But Steve," I respond. "Wouldn't this be better if YOU wrote the *Author Notes* for this week?"

Now for that secret.

Steve usually (almost always) reads these *Author Notes* before they go into the book. He's looking at my comment above about him writing the *Author Notes* and wondering just how serious I am...

<Steve here - It's always, not usually, and he's not serious is he???>

So, as a reader, if you are reading these *Author Notes* and think having Steve write a few of them would be fun, let's put that into the reviews so I have PROOF he needs to get off his ... old fashioned typewriter (that's a lie - he has a 13" MacBook Pro) and type up some notes for us to plug into these books.

Hehehehe...

<Steve here again - I've got a better idea, let's use the phrase "We LOVE Michael's author notes, don't change a thing" in all of our reviews going forward!>

Editor's Note: Resistance is futile, Steve :)

FAN PRICING

$0.99 Saturdays (new LMBPN stuff) and $0.99 Wednesday (both LMBPN books and friends of LMBPN books.) Get great stuff from us and others at tantalizing prices.

Go ahead. I bet you can't read just one.

Sign up here: http://lmbpn.com/email/.

HOW TO MARKET FOR BOOKS YOU LOVE

Review them so others have your thoughts, and tell friends and the dogs of your enemies (because who wants to talk to enemies?)... *Enough said ;-)*

Ad Aeternitatem,

Michael Anderle

OTHER BOOKS BY MARTHA CARR

Series in the Oriceran Universe:

SCHOOL OF NECESSARY MAGIC
SCHOOL OF NECESSARY MAGIC: RAINE
CAMPBELL
ALISON BROWNSTONE
THE DANIEL CODEX SERIES
THE LEIRA CHRONICLES
I FEAR NO EVIL
FEDERAL AGENTS OF MAGIC
THE UNBELIEVABLE MR. BROWNSTONE
REWRITING JUSTICE
THE KACY CHRONICLES
MIDWEST MAGIC CHRONICLES
SOUL STONE MAGE
THE FAIRHAVEN CHRONICLES

Other series:

THE LAST VAMPIRE

OTHER BOOKS BY JUDITH BERENS

OTHER BOOKS BY MARTHA CARR

JOIN THE ORICERAN UNIVERSE FAN GROUP ON FACEBOOK!

BOOKS BY MICHAEL ANDERLE

For a complete list of books by Michael Anderle, please visit

www.lmbpn.com/ma-books/

All LMBPN Audiobooks are Available at Audible.com and iTunes. For a complete list of audiobooks visit:

www.lmbpn.com/audible

CONNECT WITH THE AUTHORS

Martha Carr Social

Website: http://www.marthacarr.com

Facebook: https://www.facebook.com/
groups/MarthaCarrFans/

Michael Anderle Social

Michael Anderle Social
Website:
http://www.lmbpn.com

Email List:
http://lmbpn.com/email/

Facebook Here: https://www.
facebook.com/TheKurtherianGambitBooks/